THE QUEST FOR THE MYSTIC MOUNTAIN!

Writer: STAN LEE
Penciler: JACK KIRBY

Inker: VINCE COLLETTA
Colorist: MATT MILLA
Letterers: ART SIMEK & SAM ROSEN

Cover Artists: OLIVIER COIPEL, MARK MORALES
& LAURA MARTIN

Collection Editors: MARK D. BEAZLEY & CORY LEVINE
Assistant Editors: ALEX STARBUCK & NELSON RIBEIRO
Editor, Special Projects: JENNIFER GRÜNWALD
Senior Editor, Special Projects: JEFF YOUNGQUIST
SVP of Print & Digital Publishing Sales: DAVID GABRIEL
Research: JEPH YORK & DANA PERKINS
Select Art Reconstruction: TOM ZIUKO
Production: JERRON QUALITY COLOR & JOE FRONTIRRE
Book Designer: SPRING HOTELING

Editor In Chief: AXEL ALONSO
Chief Creative Officer: JOE QUESADA
Publisher: DAN BUCKLEY
Executive Producer: ALAN FINE

SPECIAL THANKS TO RALPH MACCHIO

Visit us at www.abdopublishing.com

Reinforced library bound editions published in 2014 by Spotlight, a division of the ABDO Group, PO Box 398166, Minneapolis, MN 55439. Spotlight produces high-quality reinforced library bound editions for schools and libraries. Published by agreement with Marvel Characters, Inc.

Printed in the United States of America, North Mankato, Minnesota.
042013
092013
This book contains at least 10% recycled material.

MARVEL

Library of Congress Cataloging-in-Publication Data

Lee, Stan.
The quest for the mystic mountain! / story by Stan Lee ; art by Jack Kirby.
pages cm. -- (Thor, tales of Asgard)
"Marvel."
Summary: An adaptation, in graphic novel form, of comic books revealing the adventures of the Norse Gods and Thor before he came to Earth, featuring a journey the godling takes to the land of Hindi, seeking the Magic Mountain of Mogul.
ISBN 978-1-61479-172-0 (alk. paper)
1. Thor (Norse deity)--Juvenile fiction. 2. Graphic novels. [1. Graphic novels. 2. Thor (Norse deity)--Fiction. 3. Mythology, Norse--Fiction.] I. Kirby, Jack, illustrator. II. Title.
PZ7.S81712Que 2013
741.5'973--dc23

2013005406

Spotlight

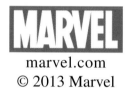

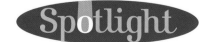

All Spotlight books are reinforced library bindings and manufactured in the United States of America.

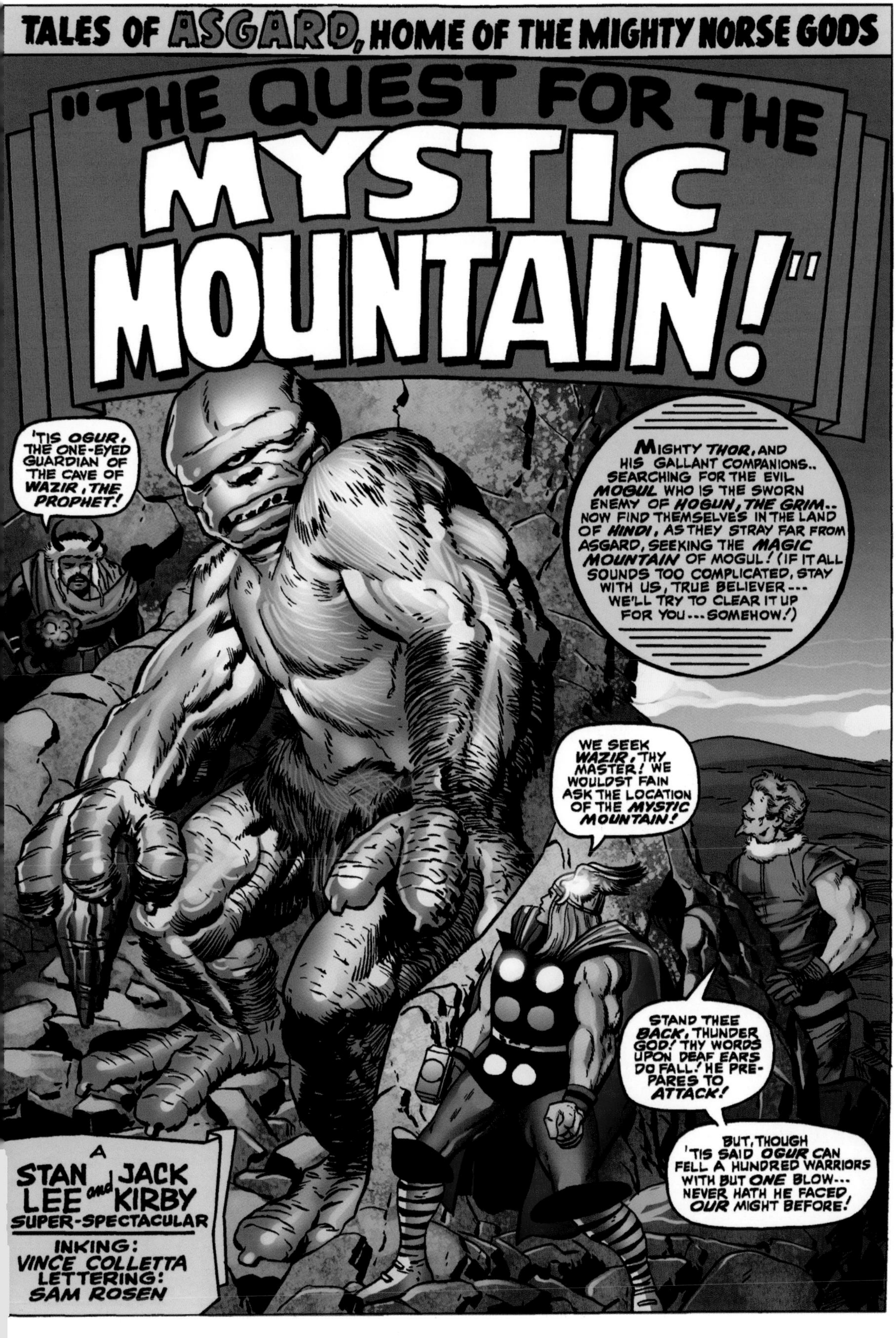

TALES OF ASGARD, HOME OF THE MIGHTY NORSE GODS
"THE QUEST FOR THE MYSTIC MOUNTAIN!"
'TIS OGUR, THE ONE-EYED GUARDIAN OF THE CAVE OF WAZIR, THE PROPHET!
MIGHTY THOR, AND HIS GALLANT COMPANIONS.. SEARCHING FOR THE EVIL MOGUL WHO IS THE SWORN ENEMY OF HOGUN, THE GRIM.. NOW FIND THEMSELVES IN THE LAND OF HINDI, AS THEY STRAY FAR FROM ASGARD, SEEKING THE MAGIC MOUNTAIN OF MOGUL! (IF IT ALL SOUNDS TOO COMPLICATED, STAY WITH US, TRUE BELIEVER--- WE'LL TRY TO CLEAR IT UP FOR YOU---SOMEHOW!)
WE SEEK WAZIR, THY MASTER! WE WOULDST FAIN ASK THE LOCATION OF THE MYSTIC MOUNTAIN!
STAND THEE BACK, THUNDER GOD! THY WORDS UPON DEAF EARS DO FALL! HE PREPARES TO ATTACK!
BUT, THOUGH 'TIS SAID OGUR CAN FELL A HUNDRED WARRIORS WITH BUT ONE BLOW--- NEVER HATH HE FACED OUR MIGHT BEFORE!
A STAN LEE and JACK KIRBY SUPER-SPECTACULAR
INKING: VINCE COLLETTA
LETTERING: SAM ROSEN

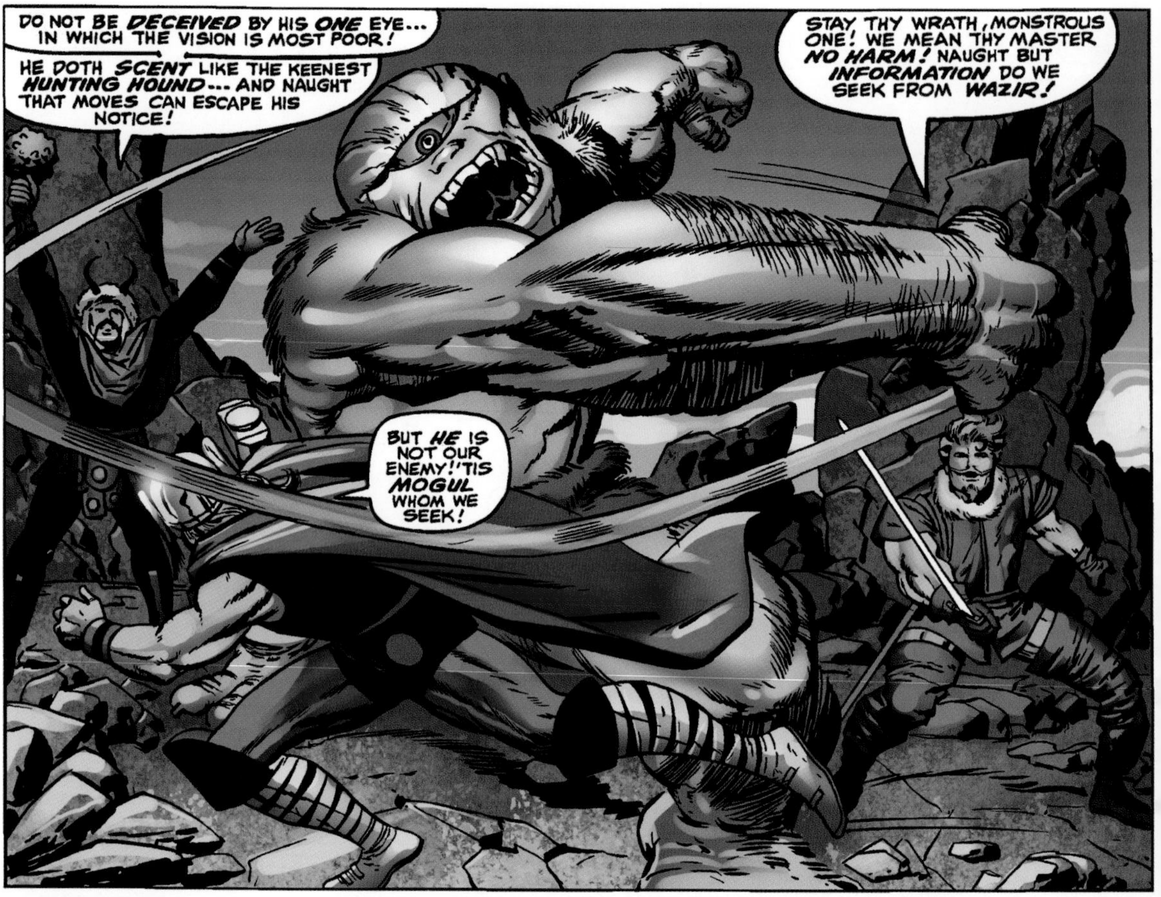
DO NOT BE DECEIVED BY HIS ONE EYE... IN WHICH THE VISION IS MOST POOR!
HE DOTH SCENT LIKE THE KEENEST HUNTING HOUND... AND NAUGHT THAT MOVES CAN ESCAPE HIS NOTICE!
STAY THY WRATH, MONSTROUS ONE! WE MEAN THY MASTER NO HARM! NAUGHT BUT INFORMATION DO WE SEEK FROM WAZIR!
BUT HE IS NOT OUR ENEMY! 'TIS MOGUL WHOM WE SEEK!

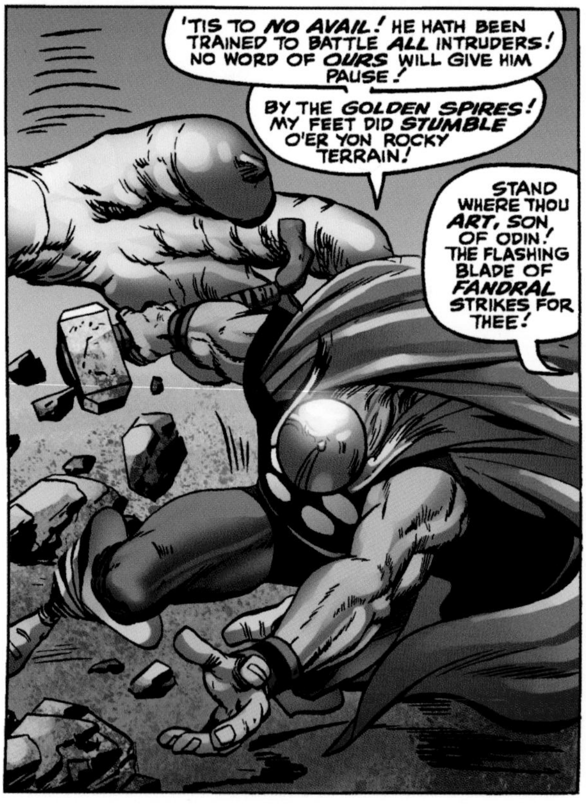
'TIS TO NO AVAIL! HE HATH BEEN TRAINED TO BATTLE ALL INTRUDERS! NO WORD OF OURS WILL GIVE HIM PAUSE!
BY THE GOLDEN SPIRES! MY FEET DID STUMBLE O'ER YON ROCKY TERRAIN!
STAND WHERE THOU ART, SON OF ODIN! THE FLASHING BLADE OF FANDRAL STRIKES FOR THEE!

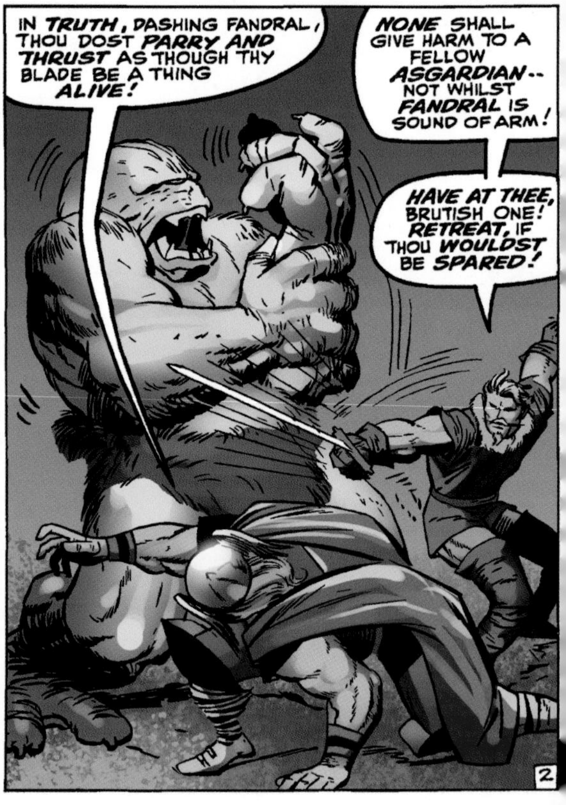
IN TRUTH, DASHING FANDRAL, THOU DOST PARRY AND THRUST AS THOUGH THY BLADE BE A THING ALIVE!
NONE SHALL GIVE HARM TO A FELLOW ASGARDIAN-- NOT WHILST FANDRAL IS SOUND OF ARM!
HAVE AT THEE, BRUTISH ONE! RETREAT, IF THOU WOULDST BE SPARED!
2

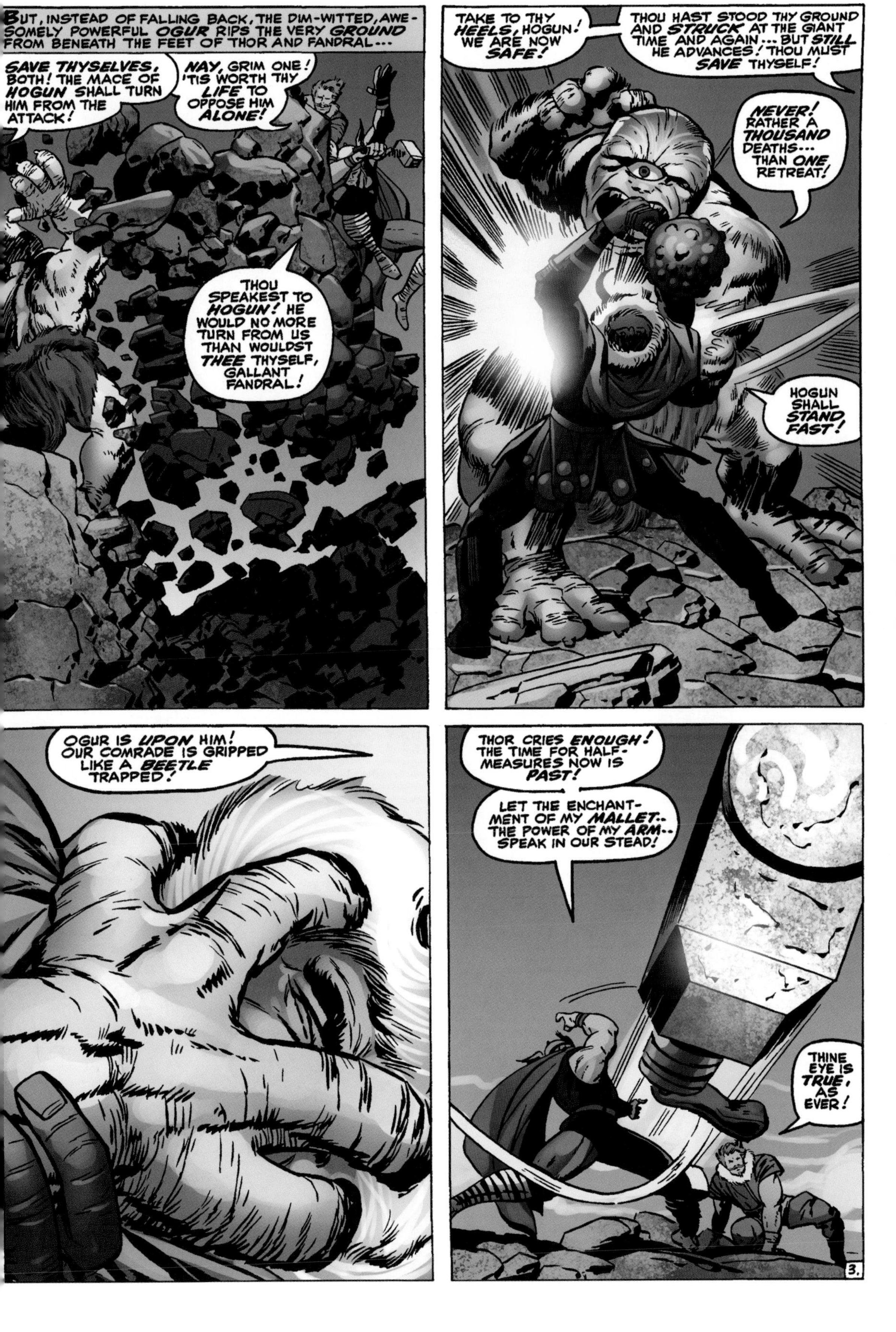
BUT, INSTEAD OF FALLING BACK, THE DIM-WITTED, AWE-SOMELY POWERFUL OGUR RIPS THE VERY GROUND FROM BENEATH THE FEET OF THOR AND FANDRAL...
SAVE THYSELVES, BOTH! THE MACE OF HOGUN SHALL TURN HIM FROM THE ATTACK!
NAY, GRIM ONE! 'TIS WORTH THY LIFE TO OPPOSE HIM ALONE!
THOU SPEAKEST TO HOGUN! HE WOULD NO MORE TURN FROM US THAN WOULDST THEE THYSELF, GALLANT FANDRAL!
TAKE TO THY HEELS, HOGUN! WE ARE NOW SAFE!
THOU HAST STOOD THY GROUND AND STRUCK AT THE GIANT TIME AND AGAIN... BUT STILL HE ADVANCES! THOU MUST SAVE THYSELF!
NEVER! RATHER A THOUSAND DEATHS... THAN ONE RETREAT!
HOGUN SHALL STAND FAST!
OGUR IS UPON HIM! OUR COMRADE IS GRIPPED LIKE A BEETLE TRAPPED!
THOR CRIES ENOUGH! THE TIME FOR HALF-MEASURES NOW IS PAST!
LET THE ENCHANTMENT OF MY MALLET.. THE POWER OF MY ARM.. SPEAK IN OUR STEAD!
THINE EYE IS TRUE, AS EVER!
3.

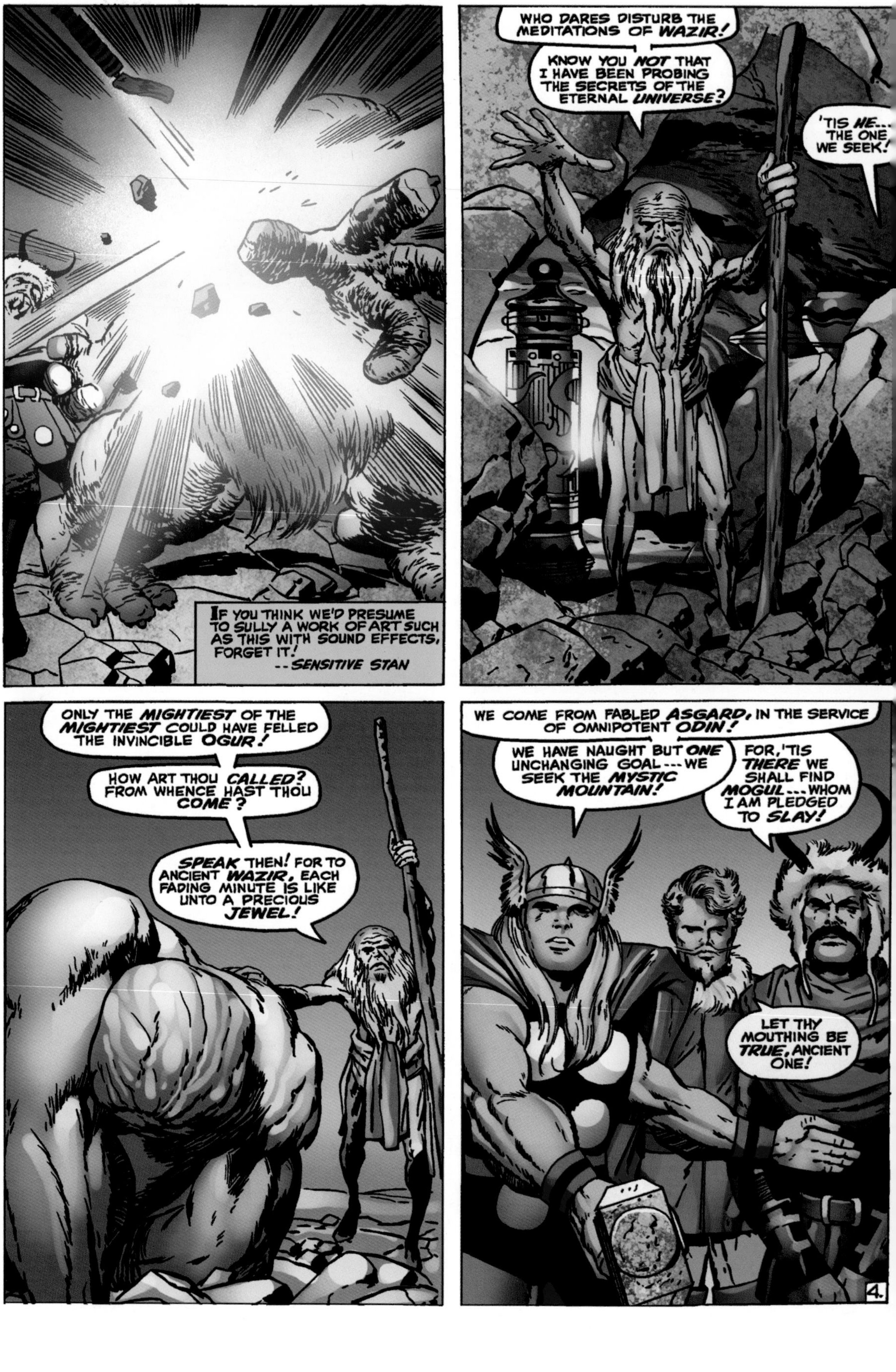
IF YOU THINK WE'D PRESUME TO SULLY A WORK OF ART SUCH AS THIS WITH SOUND EFFECTS, FORGET IT! --SENSITIVE STAN
WHO DARES DISTURB THE MEDITATIONS OF WAZIR!
KNOW YOU NOT THAT I HAVE BEEN PROBING THE SECRETS OF THE ETERNAL UNIVERSE?
'TIS HE... THE ONE WE SEEK!
ONLY THE MIGHTIEST OF THE MIGHTIEST COULD HAVE FELLED THE INVINCIBLE OGUR!
HOW ART THOU CALLED? FROM WHENCE HAST THOU COME?
SPEAK THEN! FOR TO ANCIENT WAZIR, EACH FADING MINUTE IS LIKE UNTO A PRECIOUS JEWEL!
WE COME FROM FABLED ASGARD, IN THE SERVICE OF OMNIPOTENT ODIN!
WE HAVE NAUGHT BUT ONE UNCHANGING GOAL---WE SEEK THE MYSTIC MOUNTAIN!
FOR, 'TIS THERE WE SHALL FIND MOGUL...WHOM I AM PLEDGED TO SLAY!
LET THY MOUTHING BE TRUE, ANCIENT ONE!
4.

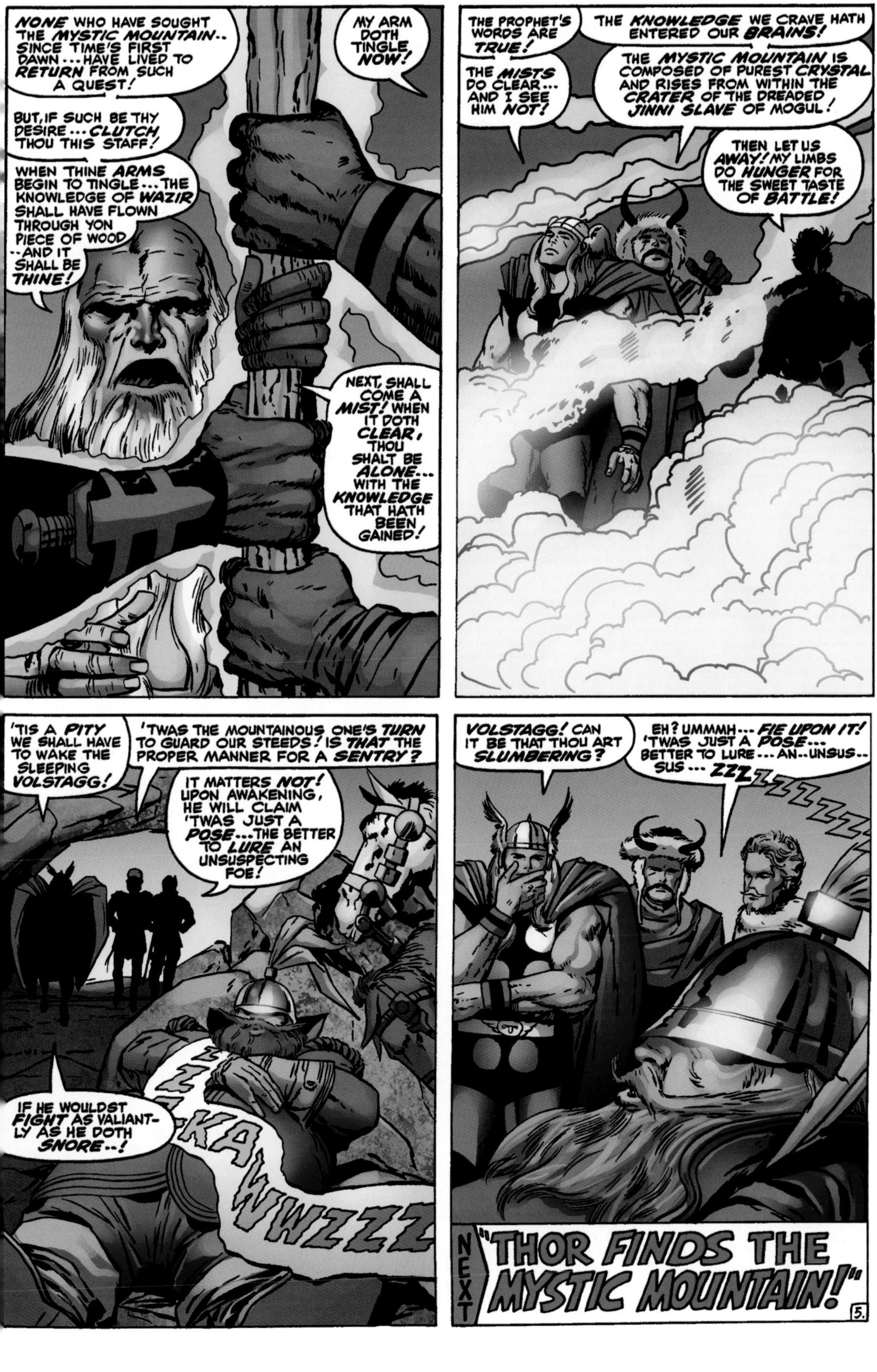
NONE WHO HAVE SOUGHT THE MYSTIC MOUNTAIN.. SINCE TIME'S FIRST DAWN... HAVE LIVED TO RETURN FROM SUCH A QUEST!
BUT, IF SUCH BE THY DESIRE... CLUTCH THOU THIS STAFF!
WHEN THINE ARMS BEGIN TO TINGLE... THE KNOWLEDGE OF WAZIR SHALL HAVE FLOWN THROUGH YON PIECE OF WOOD --AND IT SHALL BE THINE!
MY ARM DOTH TINGLE, NOW!
NEXT, SHALL COME A MIST! WHEN IT DOTH CLEAR, THOU SHALT BE ALONE... WITH THE KNOWLEDGE THAT HATH BEEN GAINED!
THE PROPHET'S WORDS ARE TRUE!
THE MISTS DO CLEAR... AND I SEE HIM NOT!
THE KNOWLEDGE WE CRAVE HATH ENTERED OUR BRAINS!
THE MYSTIC MOUNTAIN IS COMPOSED OF PUREST CRYSTAL AND RISES FROM WITHIN THE CRATER OF THE DREADED JINNI SLAVE OF MOGUL!
THEN LET US AWAY! MY LIMBS DO HUNGER FOR THE SWEET TASTE OF BATTLE!
'TIS A PITY WE SHALL HAVE TO WAKE THE SLEEPING VOLSTAGG!
'TWAS THE MOUNTAINOUS ONE'S TURN TO GUARD OUR STEEDS! IS THAT THE PROPER MANNER FOR A SENTRY?
IT MATTERS NOT! UPON AWAKENING, HE WILL CLAIM 'TWAS JUST A POSE... THE BETTER TO LURE AN UNSUSPECTING FOE!
IF HE WOULDST FIGHT AS VALIANTLY AS HE DOTH SNORE..!
KAWWZZZ
VOLSTAGG! CAN IT BE THAT THOU ART SLUMBERING?
EH? UMMMH... FIE UPON IT! 'TWAS JUST A POSE... BETTER TO LURE... AN..UNSUS... SUS... ZZZ
NEXT "THOR FINDS THE MYSTIC MOUNTAIN!"
5.

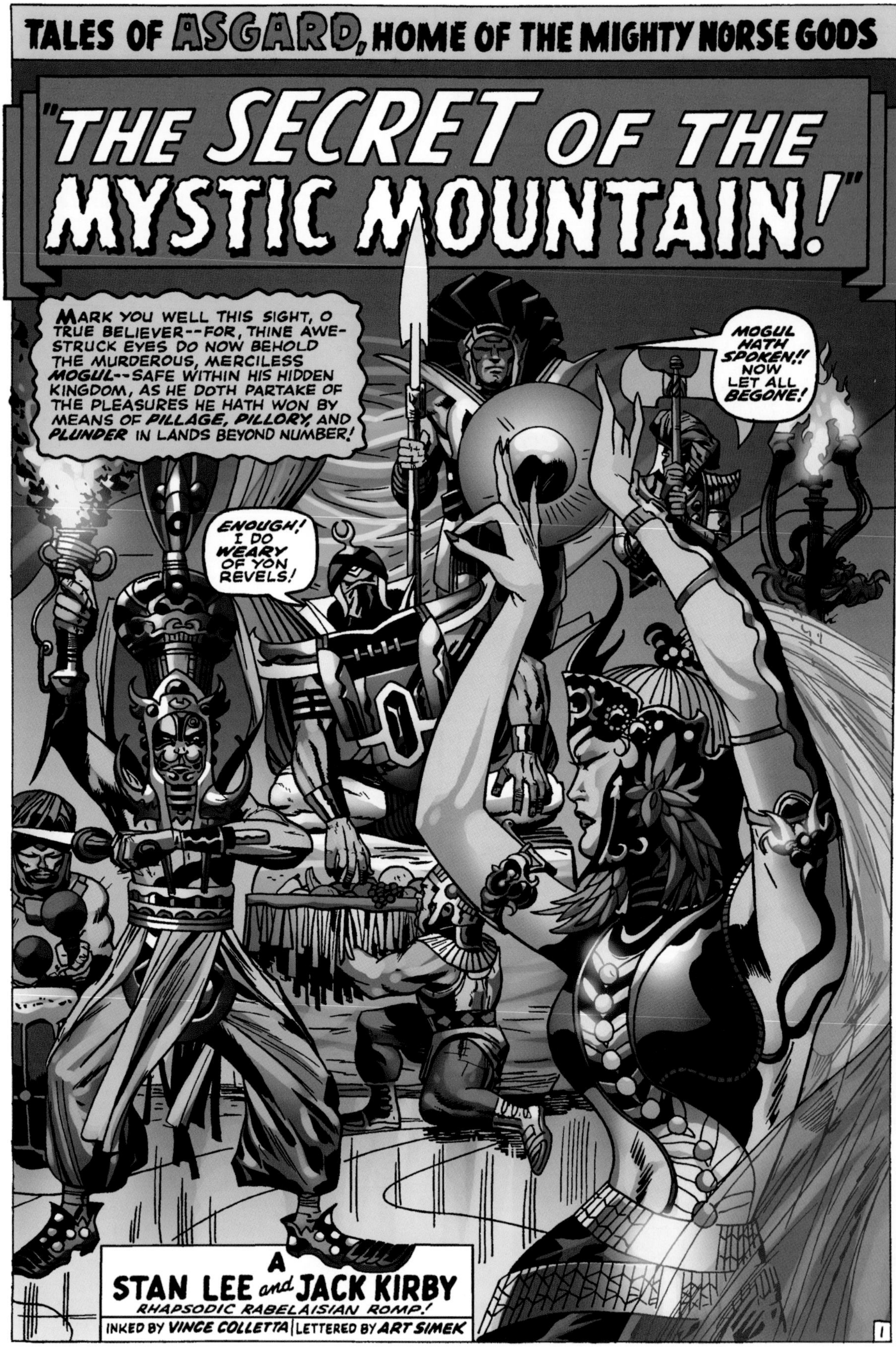
TALES OF ASGARD, HOME OF THE MIGHTY NORSE GODS
"THE SECRET OF THE MYSTIC MOUNTAIN!"
MARK YOU WELL THIS SIGHT, O TRUE BELIEVER--FOR, THINE AWE-STRUCK EYES DO NOW BEHOLD THE MURDEROUS, MERCILESS MOGUL--SAFE WITHIN HIS HIDDEN KINGDOM, AS HE DOTH PARTAKE OF THE PLEASURES HE HATH WON BY MEANS OF PILLAGE, PILLORY, AND PLUNDER IN LANDS BEYOND NUMBER!
ENOUGH! I DO WEARY OF YON REVELS!
MOGUL HATH SPOKEN!! NOW LET ALL BEGONE!
A STAN LEE and JACK KIRBY RHAPSODIC RABELAISIAN ROMP!
INKED BY VINCE COLLETTA | LETTERED BY ART SIMEK
1

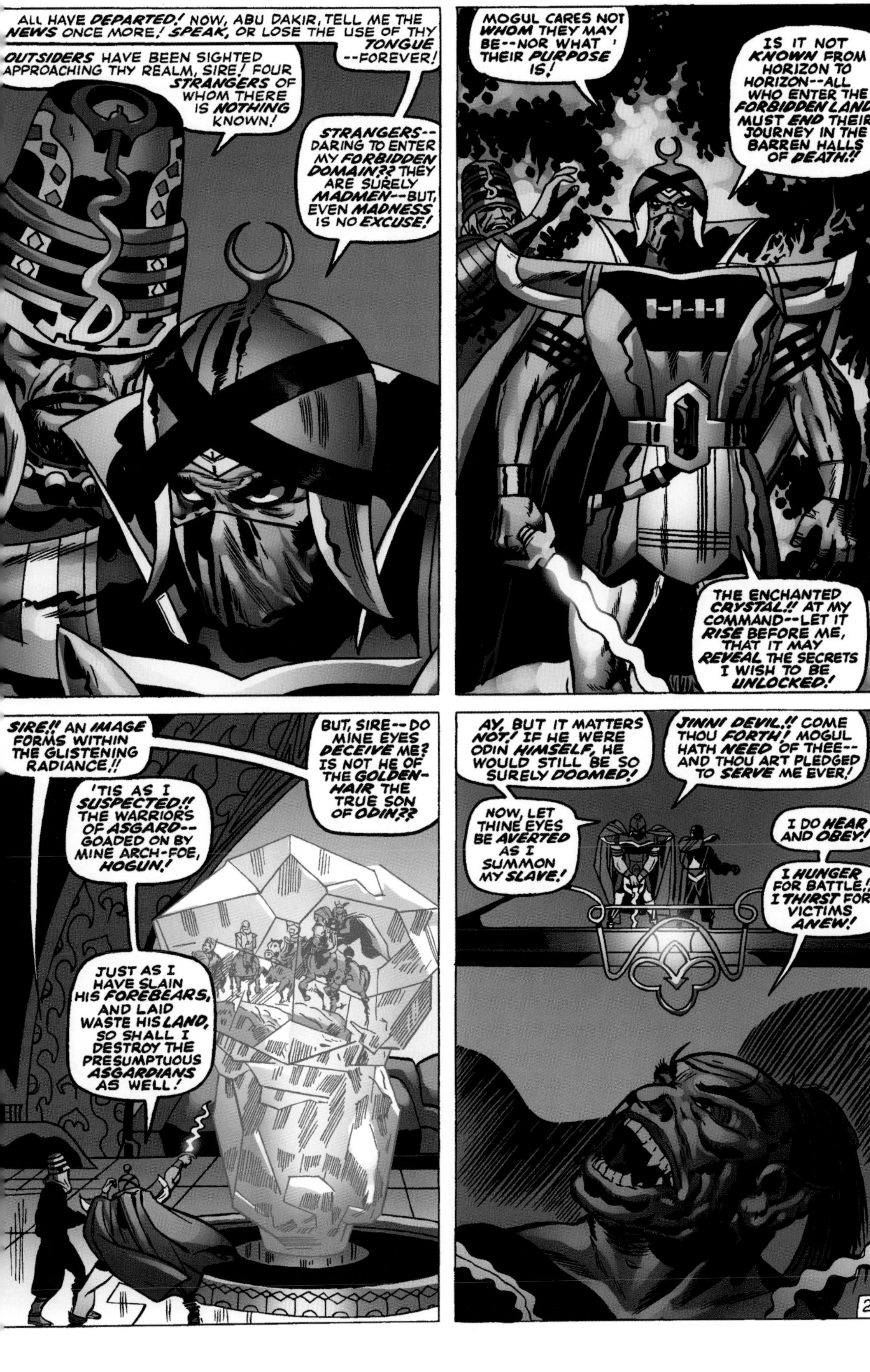
ALL HAVE DEPARTED! NOW, ABU DAKIR, TELL ME THE NEWS ONCE MORE! SPEAK, OR LOSE THE USE OF THY TONGUE --FOREVER!
OUTSIDERS HAVE BEEN SIGHTED APPROACHING THY REALM, SIRE! FOUR STRANGERS OF WHOM THERE IS NOTHING KNOWN!
STRANGERS-- DARING TO ENTER MY FORBIDDEN DOMAIN?? THEY ARE SURELY MADMEN--BUT, EVEN MADNESS IS NO EXCUSE!
MOGUL CARES NOT WHOM THEY MAY BE--NOR WHAT THEIR PURPOSE IS!
IS IT NOT KNOWN FROM HORIZON TO HORIZON--ALL WHO ENTER THE FORBIDDEN LAND MUST END THEIR JOURNEY IN THE BARREN HALLS OF DEATH!!
THE ENCHANTED CRYSTAL!! AT MY COMMAND--LET IT RISE BEFORE ME, THAT IT MAY REVEAL THE SECRETS I WISH TO BE UNLOCKED!
SIRE!! AN IMAGE FORMS WITHIN THE GLISTENING RADIANCE!!
'TIS AS I SUSPECTED!! THE WARRIORS OF ASGARD-- GOADED ON BY MINE ARCH-FOE, HOGUN!
BUT, SIRE--DO MINE EYES DECEIVE ME? IS NOT HE OF THE GOLDEN-HAIR THE TRUE SON OF ODIN??
JUST AS I HAVE SLAIN HIS FOREBEARS, AND LAID WASTE HIS LAND, SO SHALL I DESTROY THE PRESUMPTUOUS ASGARDIANS AS WELL!
AY, BUT IT MATTERS NOT! IF HE WERE ODIN HIMSELF, HE WOULD STILL BE SO SURELY DOOMED!
NOW, LET THINE EYES BE AVERTED AS I SUMMON MY SLAVE!
JINNI DEVIL!! COME THOU FORTH! MOGUL HATH NEED OF THEE-- AND THOU ART PLEDGED TO SERVE ME EVER!
I DO HEAR AND OBEY!
I HUNGER FOR BATTLE!! I THIRST FOR VICTIMS ANEW!
2

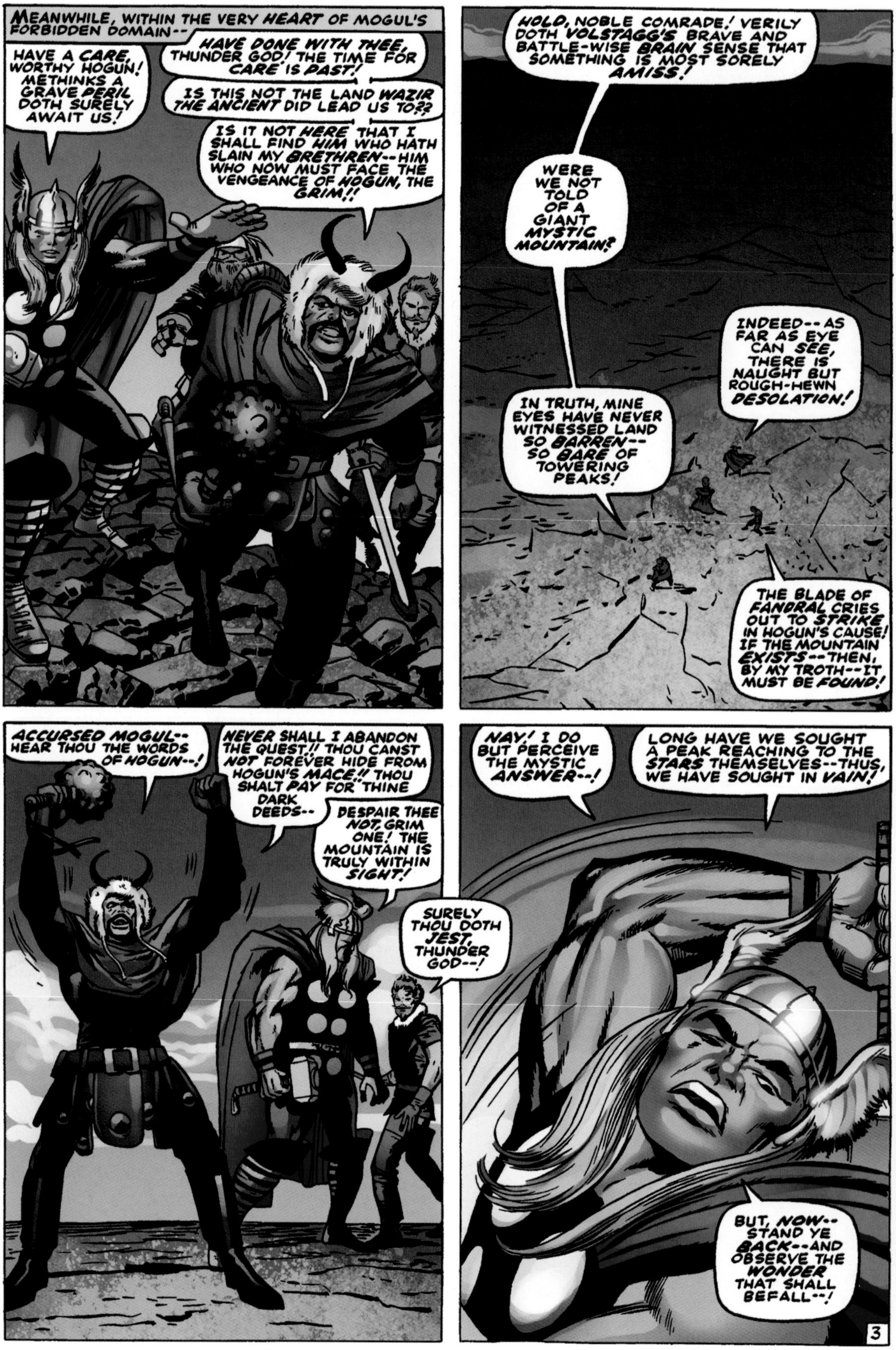
MEANWHILE, WITHIN THE VERY HEART OF MOGUL'S FORBIDDEN DOMAIN--
HAVE A CARE, WORTHY HOGUN! METHINKS A GRAVE PERIL DOTH SURELY AWAIT US!
HAVE DONE WITH THEE, THUNDER GOD! THE TIME FOR CARE IS PAST!
IS THIS NOT THE LAND WAZIR THE ANCIENT DID LEAD US TO??
IS IT NOT HERE THAT I SHALL FIND HIM WHO HATH SLAIN MY BRETHREN--HIM WHO NOW MUST FACE THE VENGEANCE OF HOGUN, THE GRIM!!
HOLD, NOBLE COMRADE! VERILY DOTH VOLSTAGG'S BRAVE AND BATTLE-WISE BRAIN SENSE THAT SOMETHING IS MOST SORELY AMISS!
WERE WE NOT TOLD OF A GIANT MYSTIC MOUNTAIN?
IN TRUTH, MINE EYES HAVE NEVER WITNESSED LAND SO BARREN--SO BARE OF TOWERING PEAKS!
INDEED--AS FAR AS EYE CAN SEE, THERE IS NAUGHT BUT ROUGH-HEWN DESOLATION!
THE BLADE OF FANDRAL CRIES OUT TO STRIKE IN HOGUN'S CAUSE! IF THE MOUNTAIN EXISTS--THEN, BY MY TROTH--IT MUST BE FOUND!
ACCURSED MOGUL--HEAR THOU THE WORDS OF HOGUN--!
NEVER SHALL I ABANDON THE QUEST!! THOU CANST NOT FOREVER HIDE FROM HOGUN'S MACE!! THOU SHALT PAY FOR THINE DARK DEEDS--
DESPAIR THEE NOT, GRIM ONE! THE MOUNTAIN IS TRULY WITHIN SIGHT!
SURELY THOU DOTH JEST, THUNDER GOD--!
NAY! I DO BUT PERCEIVE THE MYSTIC ANSWER--!
LONG HAVE WE SOUGHT A PEAK REACHING TO THE STARS THEMSELVES--THUS, WE HAVE SOUGHT IN VAIN!
BUT, NOW--STAND YE BACK--AND OBSERVE THE WONDER THAT SHALL BEFALL--!
3

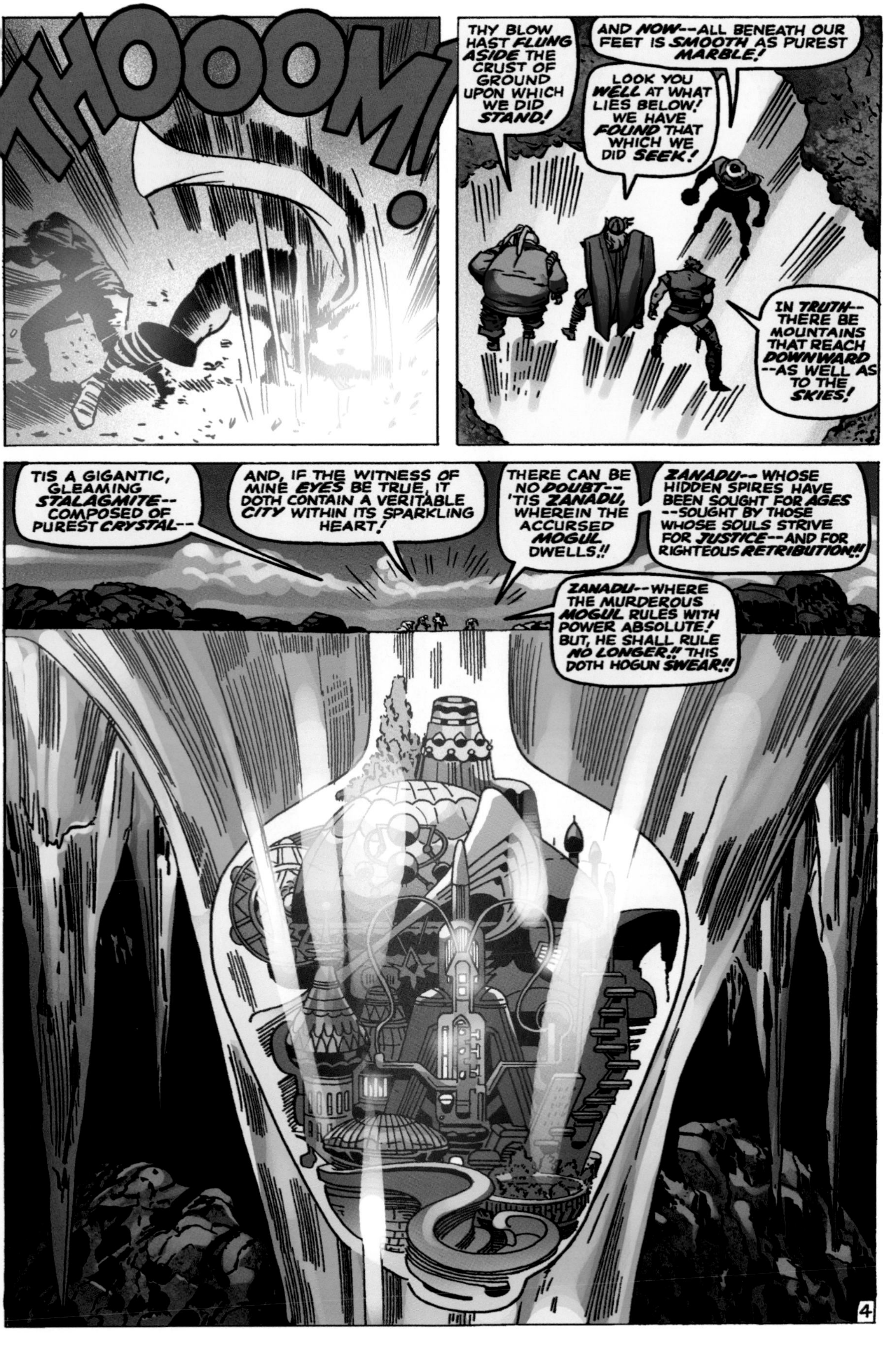
THOOOM!
THY BLOW HAST FLUNG ASIDE THE CRUST OF GROUND UPON WHICH WE DID STAND!
AND NOW--ALL BENEATH OUR FEET IS SMOOTH AS PUREST MARBLE!
LOOK YOU WELL AT WHAT LIES BELOW! WE HAVE FOUND THAT WHICH WE DID SEEK!
IN TRUTH--THERE BE MOUNTAINS THAT REACH DOWNWARD--AS WELL AS TO THE SKIES!
TIS A GIGANTIC, GLEAMING STALAGMITE--COMPOSED OF PUREST CRYSTAL--
AND, IF THE WITNESS OF MINE EYES BE TRUE, IT DOTH CONTAIN A VERITABLE CITY WITHIN ITS SPARKLING HEART!
THERE CAN BE NO DOUBT--'TIS ZANADU, WHEREIN THE ACCURSED MOGUL DWELLS!!
ZANADU--WHOSE HIDDEN SPIRES HAVE BEEN SOUGHT FOR AGES--SOUGHT BY THOSE WHOSE SOULS STRIVE FOR JUSTICE--AND FOR RIGHTEOUS RETRIBUTION!!
ZANADU--WHERE THE MURDEROUS MOGUL RULES WITH POWER ABSOLUTE! BUT, HE SHALL RULE NO LONGER!! THIS DOTH HOGUN SWEAR!!
4

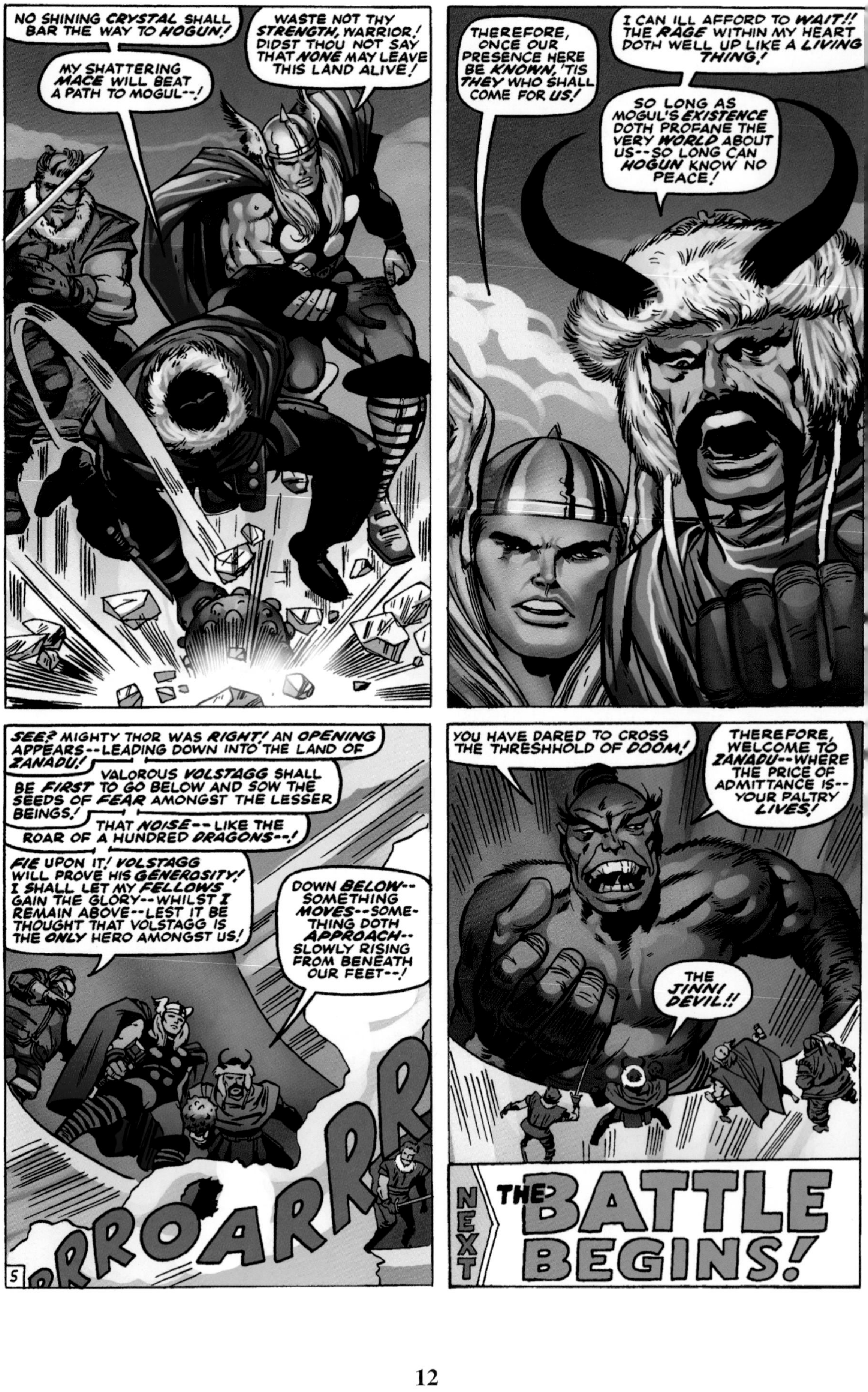
NO SHINING CRYSTAL SHALL BAR THE WAY TO HOGUN!
MY SHATTERING MACE WILL BEAT A PATH TO MOGUL--!
WASTE NOT THY STRENGTH, WARRIOR! DIDST THOU NOT SAY THAT NONE MAY LEAVE THIS LAND ALIVE!
THEREFORE, ONCE OUR PRESENCE HERE BE KNOWN, 'TIS THEY WHO SHALL COME FOR US!
I CAN ILL AFFORD TO WAIT!! THE RAGE WITHIN MY HEART DOTH WELL UP LIKE A LIVING THING!
SO LONG AS MOGUL'S EXISTENCE DOTH PROFANE THE VERY WORLD ABOUT US--SO LONG CAN HOGUN KNOW NO PEACE!
SEE? MIGHTY THOR WAS RIGHT! AN OPENING APPEARS--LEADING DOWN INTO THE LAND OF ZANADU!
VALOROUS VOLSTAGG SHALL BE FIRST TO GO BELOW AND SOW THE SEEDS OF FEAR AMONGST THE LESSER BEINGS!
THAT NOISE-- LIKE THE ROAR OF A HUNDRED DRAGONS--!
FIE UPON IT! VOLSTAGG WILL PROVE HIS GENEROSITY! I SHALL LET MY FELLOWS GAIN THE GLORY--WHILST I REMAIN ABOVE--LEST IT BE THOUGHT THAT VOLSTAGG IS THE ONLY HERO AMONGST US!
DOWN BELOW--SOMETHING MOVES--SOMETHING DOTH APPROACH--SLOWLY RISING FROM BENEATH OUR FEET--!
RRROARRR
5
YOU HAVE DARED TO CROSS THE THRESHHOLD OF DOOM!
THEREFORE, WELCOME TO ZANADU--WHERE THE PRICE OF ADMITTANCE IS--YOUR PALTRY LIVES!
THE JINNI DEVIL!!
NEXT
THE BATTLE BEGINS!

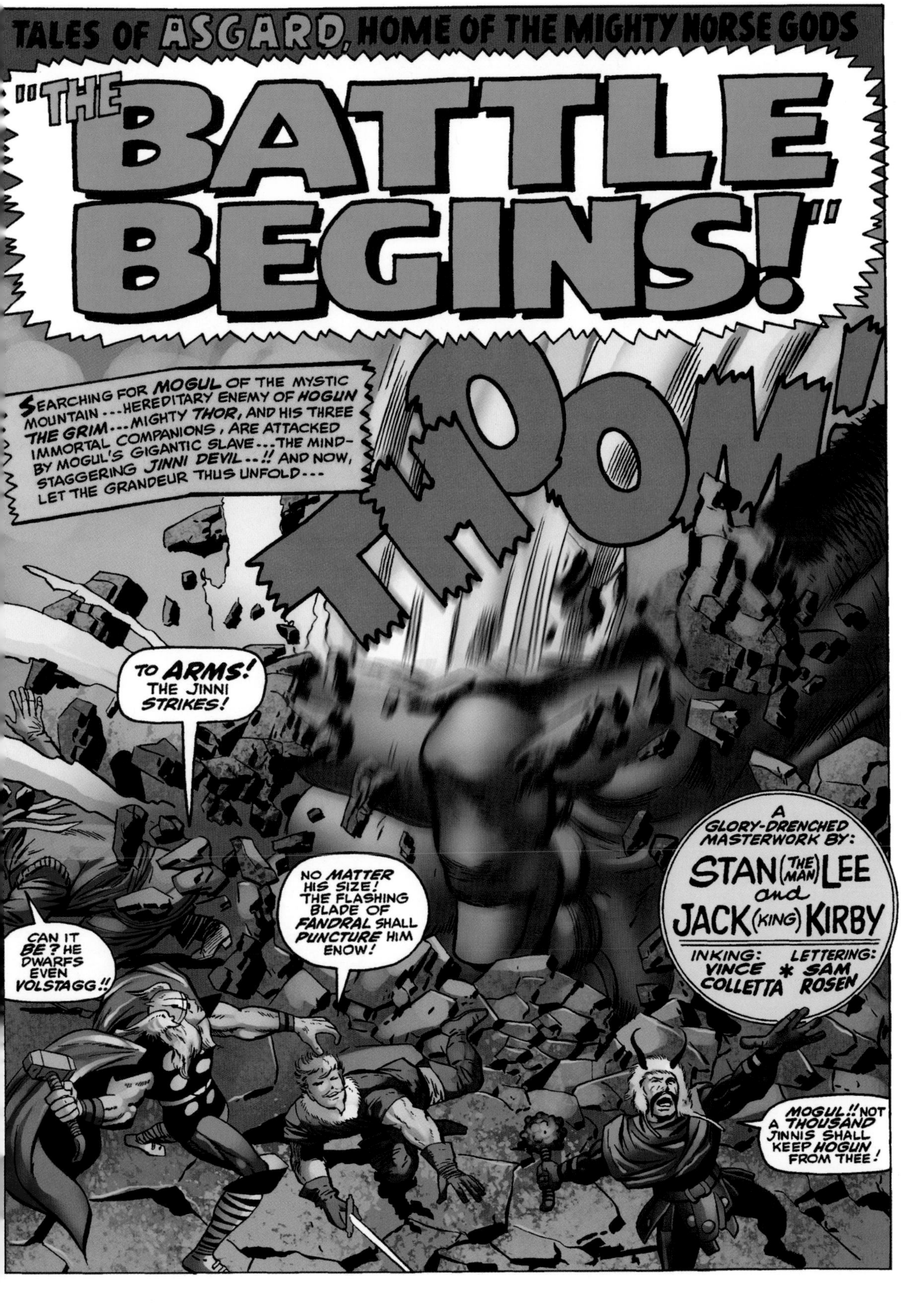
TALES OF ASGARD, HOME OF THE MIGHTY NORSE GODS
"THE BATTLE BEGINS!"
SEARCHING FOR MOGUL OF THE MYSTIC MOUNTAIN---HEREDITARY ENEMY OF HOGUN THE GRIM---MIGHTY THOR, AND HIS THREE IMMORTAL COMPANIONS, ARE ATTACKED BY MOGUL'S GIGANTIC SLAVE---THE MIND-STAGGERING JINNI DEVIL--!! AND NOW, LET THE GRANDEUR THUS UNFOLD---
THOOM!
TO ARMS! THE JINNI STRIKES!
A GLORY-DRENCHED MASTERWORK BY: STAN (THE MAN) LEE and JACK (KING) KIRBY
INKING: VINCE COLLETTA * LETTERING: SAM ROSEN
NO MATTER HIS SIZE! THE FLASHING BLADE OF FANDRAL SHALL PUNCTURE HIM ENOW!
CAN IT BE? HE DWARFS EVEN VOLSTAGG!!
MOGUL!! NOT A THOUSAND JINNIS SHALL KEEP HOGUN FROM THEE!

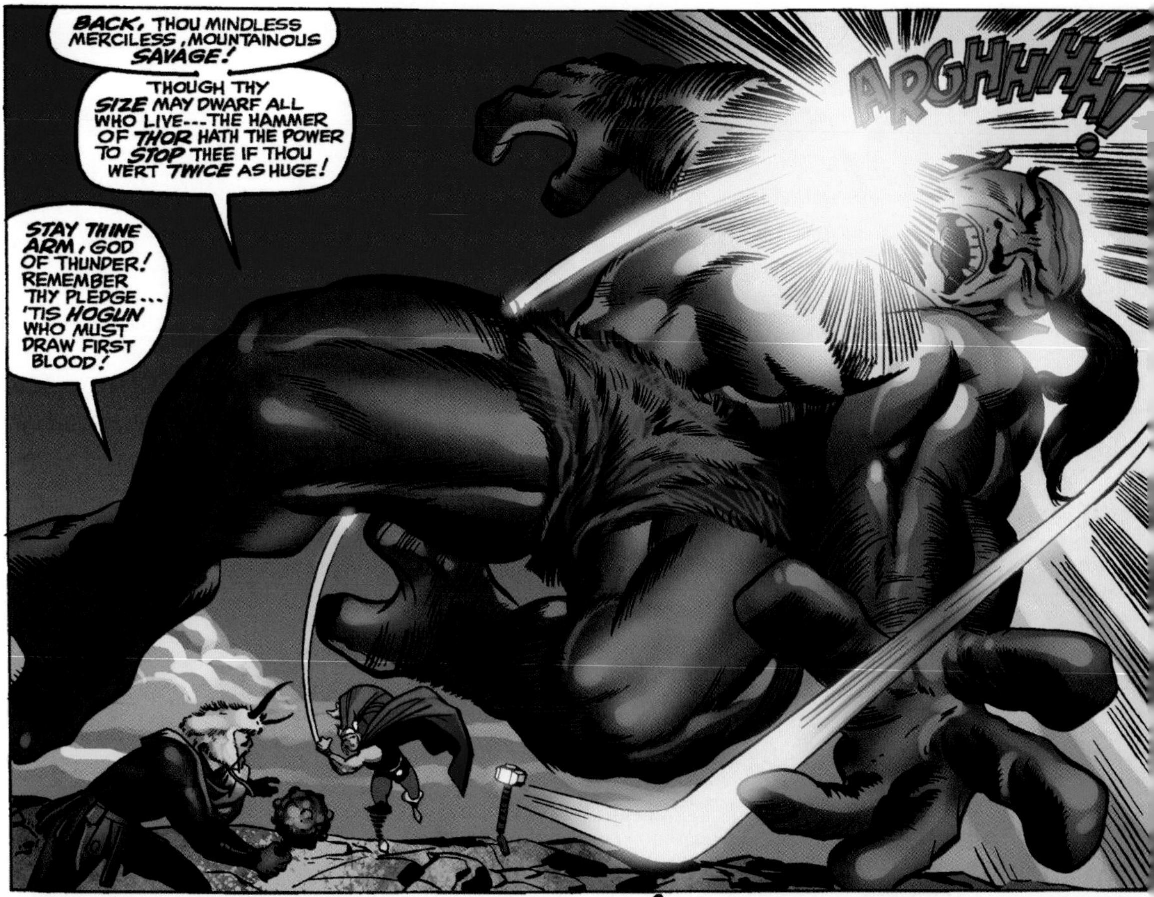
BACK, THOU MINDLESS MERCILESS, MOUNTAINOUS SAVAGE!
THOUGH THY SIZE MAY DWARF ALL WHO LIVE---THE HAMMER OF THOR HATH THE POWER TO STOP THEE IF THOU WERT TWICE AS HUGE!
ARGHHHH!
STAY THINE ARM, GOD OF THUNDER! REMEMBER THY PLEDGE... 'TIS HOGUN WHO MUST DRAW FIRST BLOOD!
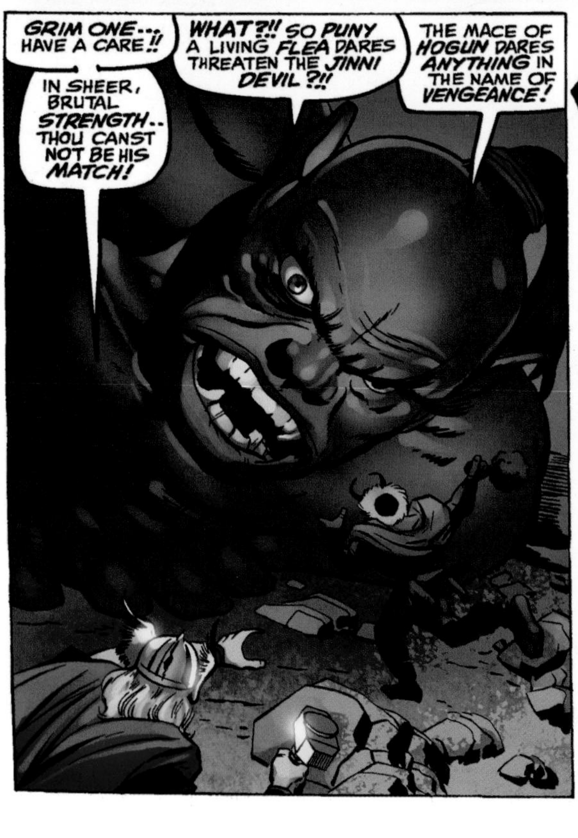
GRIM ONE--, HAVE A CARE!!
IN SHEER, BRUTAL STRENGTH.. THOU CANST NOT BE HIS MATCH!
WHAT?!! SO PUNY A LIVING FLEA DARES THREATEN THE JINNI DEVIL?!!
THE MACE OF HOGUN DARES ANYTHING IN THE NAME OF VENGEANCE!
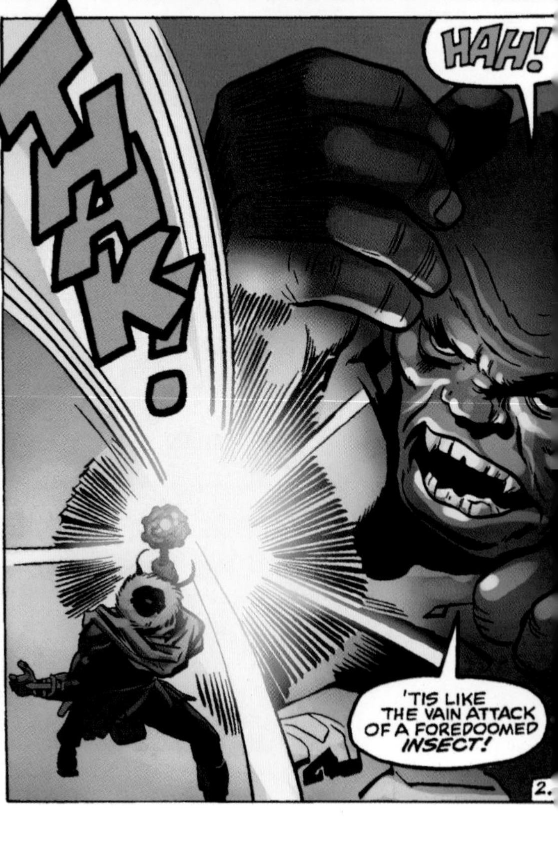
THAK!
HAH!
'TIS LIKE THE VAIN ATTACK OF A FOREDOOMED INSECT!
2.

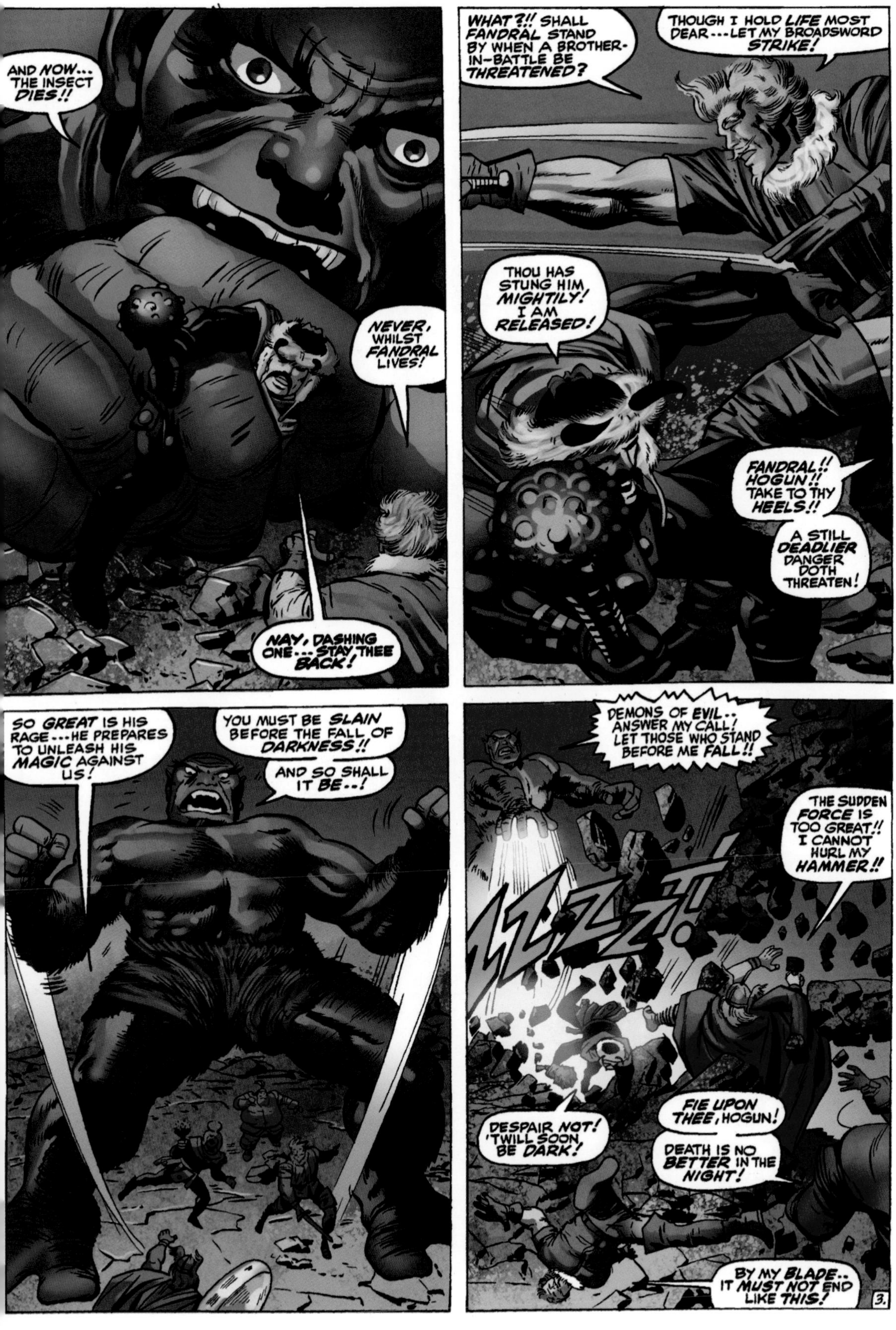
AND NOW... THE INSECT DIES!!
NEVER, WHILST FANDRAL LIVES!
NAY, DASHING ONE... STAY THEE BACK!
WHAT?!! SHALL FANDRAL STAND BY WHEN A BROTHER-IN-BATTLE BE THREATENED?
THOUGH I HOLD LIFE MOST DEAR---LET MY BROADSWORD STRIKE!
THOU HAS STUNG HIM MIGHTILY! I AM RELEASED!
FANDRAL!! HOGUN!! TAKE TO THY HEELS!!
A STILL DEADLIER DANGER DOTH THREATEN!
SO GREAT IS HIS RAGE---HE PREPARES TO UNLEASH HIS MAGIC AGAINST US!
YOU MUST BE SLAIN BEFORE THE FALL OF DARKNESS!!
AND SO SHALL IT BE--!
DEMONS OF EVIL.. ANSWER MY CALL! LET THOSE WHO STAND BEFORE ME FALL!!
THE SUDDEN FORCE IS TOO GREAT!! I CANNOT HURL MY HAMMER!!
ZZZZT!
DESPAIR NOT! 'TWILL SOON BE DARK!
FIE UPON THEE, HOGUN!
DEATH IS NO BETTER IN THE NIGHT!
BY MY BLADE.. IT MUST NOT END LIKE THIS!
3.

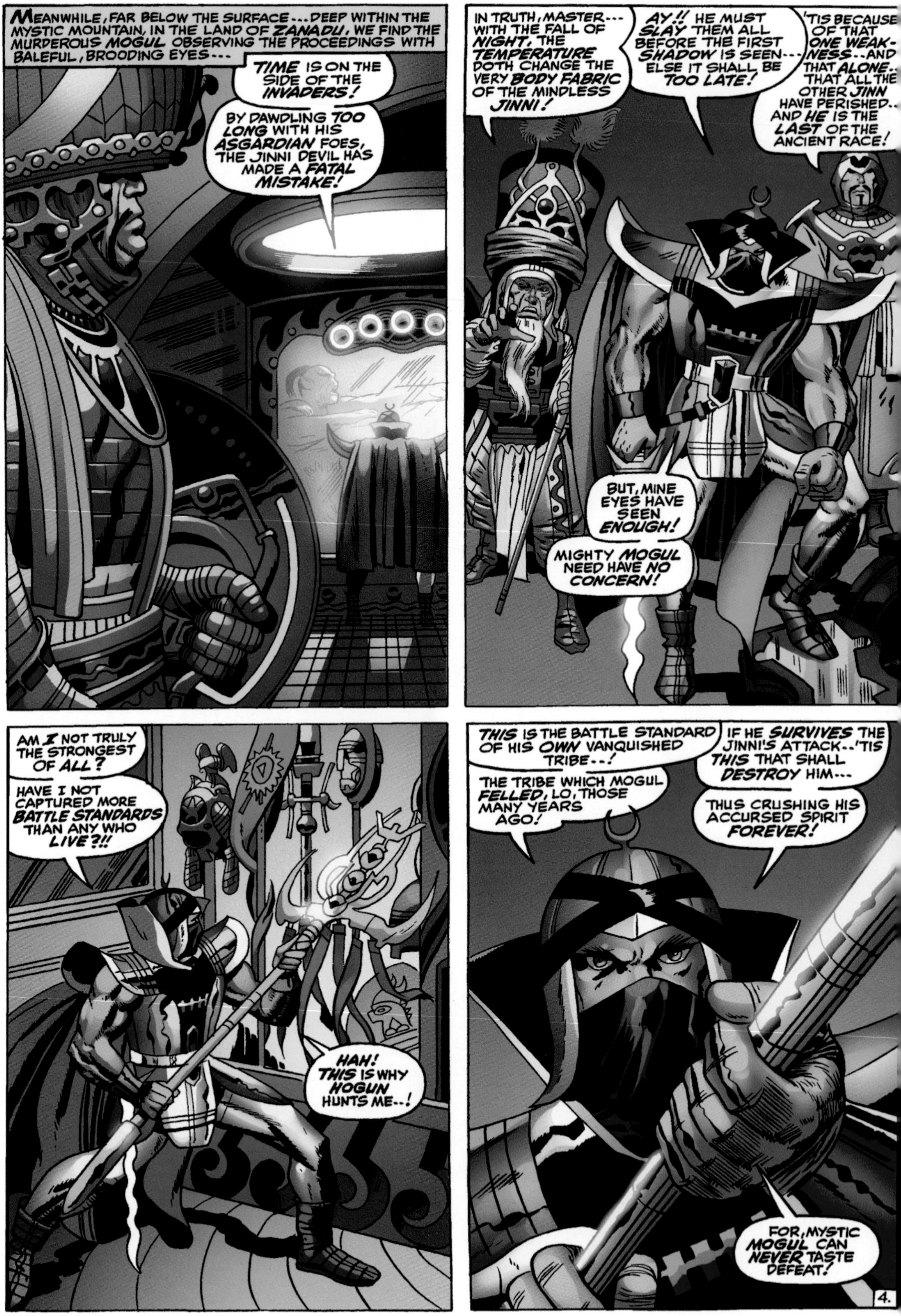
MEANWHILE, FAR BELOW THE SURFACE... DEEP WITHIN THE MYSTIC MOUNTAIN, IN THE LAND OF ZANADU, WE FIND THE MURDEROUS MOGUL OBSERVING THE PROCEEDINGS WITH BALEFUL, BROODING EYES...
TIME IS ON THE SIDE OF THE INVADERS!
BY DAWDLING TOO LONG WITH HIS ASGARDIAN FOES, THE JINNI DEVIL HAS MADE A FATAL MISTAKE!
IN TRUTH, MASTER--- WITH THE FALL OF NIGHT, THE TEMPERATURE DOTH CHANGE THE VERY BODY FABRIC OF THE MINDLESS JINNI!
AY!! HE MUST SLAY THEM ALL BEFORE THE FIRST SHADOW IS SEEN--- ELSE IT SHALL BE TOO LATE!
'TIS BECAUSE OF THAT ONE WEAKNESS..AND THAT ALONE.. THAT ALL THE OTHER JINN HAVE PERISHED.. AND HE IS THE LAST OF THE ANCIENT RACE!
BUT, MINE EYES HAVE SEEN ENOUGH!
MIGHTY MOGUL NEED HAVE NO CONCERN!
AM I NOT TRULY THE STRONGEST OF ALL?
HAVE I NOT CAPTURED MORE BATTLE STANDARDS THAN ANY WHO LIVE?!!
HAH! THIS IS WHY HOGUN HUNTS ME..!
THIS IS THE BATTLE STANDARD OF HIS OWN VANQUISHED TRIBE..!
THE TRIBE WHICH MOGUL FELLED, LO, THOSE MANY YEARS AGO!
IF HE SURVIVES THE JINNI'S ATTACK..'TIS THIS THAT SHALL DESTROY HIM...
THUS CRUSHING HIS ACCURSED SPIRIT FOREVER!
FOR, MYSTIC MOGUL CAN NEVER TASTE DEFEAT!
4.

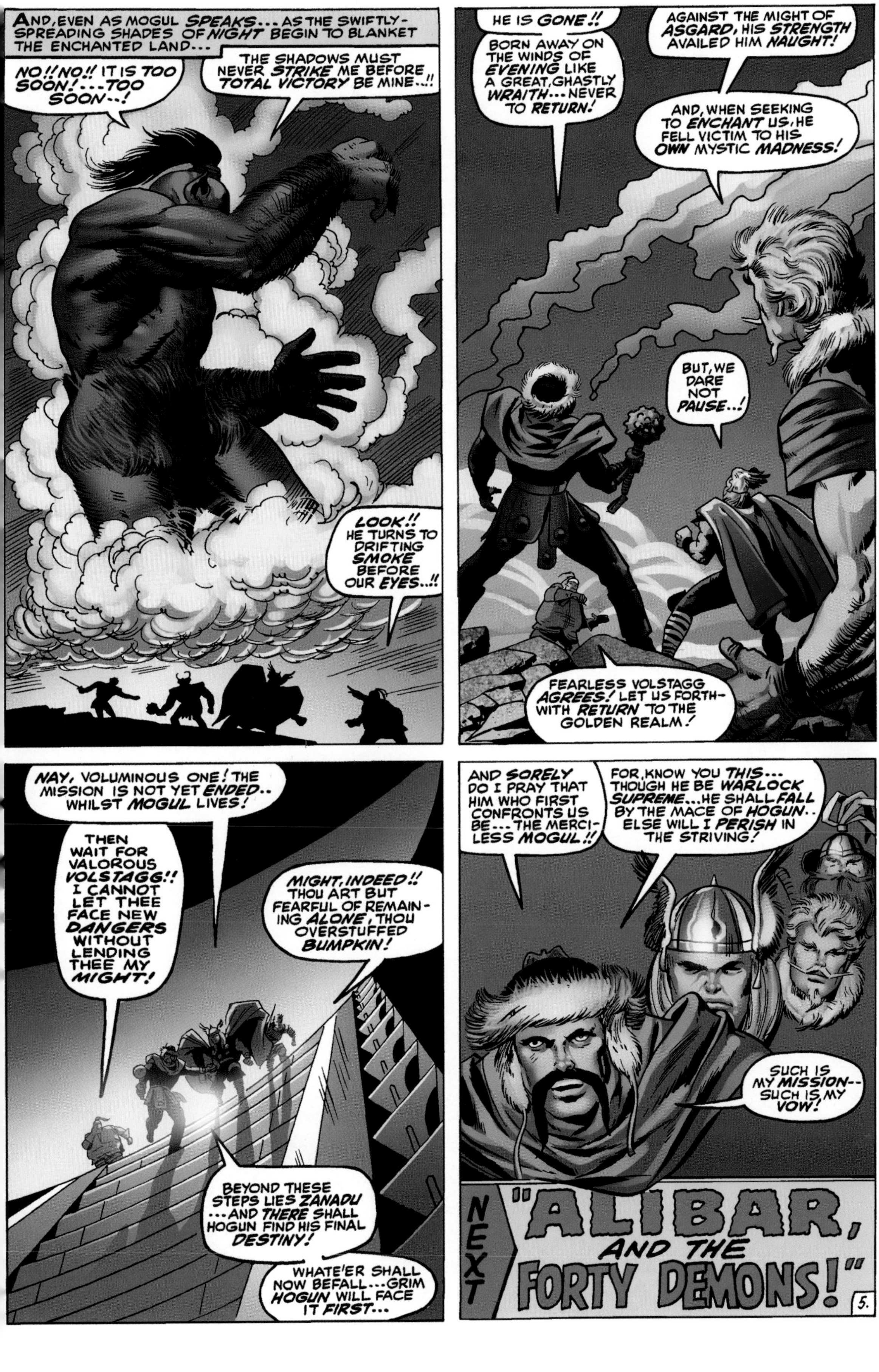
AND, EVEN AS MOGUL SPEAKS... AS THE SWIFTLY-SPREADING SHADES OF NIGHT BEGIN TO BLANKET THE ENCHANTED LAND...
NO!! NO!! IT IS TOO SOON! ...TOO SOON--!
THE SHADOWS MUST NEVER STRIKE ME BEFORE TOTAL VICTORY BE MINE--!!
LOOK!! HE TURNS TO DRIFTING SMOKE BEFORE OUR EYES...!!
HE IS GONE!!
BORN AWAY ON THE WINDS OF EVENING LIKE A GREAT, GHASTLY WRAITH... NEVER TO RETURN!
AGAINST THE MIGHT OF ASGARD, HIS STRENGTH AVAILED HIM NAUGHT!
AND, WHEN SEEKING TO ENCHANT US, HE FELL VICTIM TO HIS OWN MYSTIC MADNESS!
BUT, WE DARE NOT PAUSE...!
FEARLESS VOLSTAGG AGREES! LET US FORTHWITH RETURN TO THE GOLDEN REALM!
NAY, VOLUMINOUS ONE! THE MISSION IS NOT YET ENDED.. WHILST MOGUL LIVES!
THEN WAIT FOR VALOROUS VOLSTAGG!! I CANNOT LET THEE FACE NEW DANGERS WITHOUT LENDING THEE MY MIGHT!
MIGHT, INDEED!! THOU ART BUT FEARFUL OF REMAINING ALONE, THOU OVERSTUFFED BUMPKIN!
BEYOND THESE STEPS LIES ZANADU ...AND THERE SHALL HOGUN FIND HIS FINAL DESTINY!
WHATE'ER SHALL NOW BEFALL... GRIM HOGUN WILL FACE IT FIRST...
AND SORELY DO I PRAY THAT HIM WHO FIRST CONFRONTS US BE... THE MERCILESS MOGUL!!
FOR, KNOW YOU THIS... THOUGH HE BE WARLOCK SUPREME... HE SHALL FALL BY THE MACE OF HOGUN.. ELSE WILL I PERISH IN THE STRIVING!
SUCH IS MY MISSION-- SUCH IS MY VOW!
NEXT "ALIBAR, AND THE FORTY DEMONS!"
5.

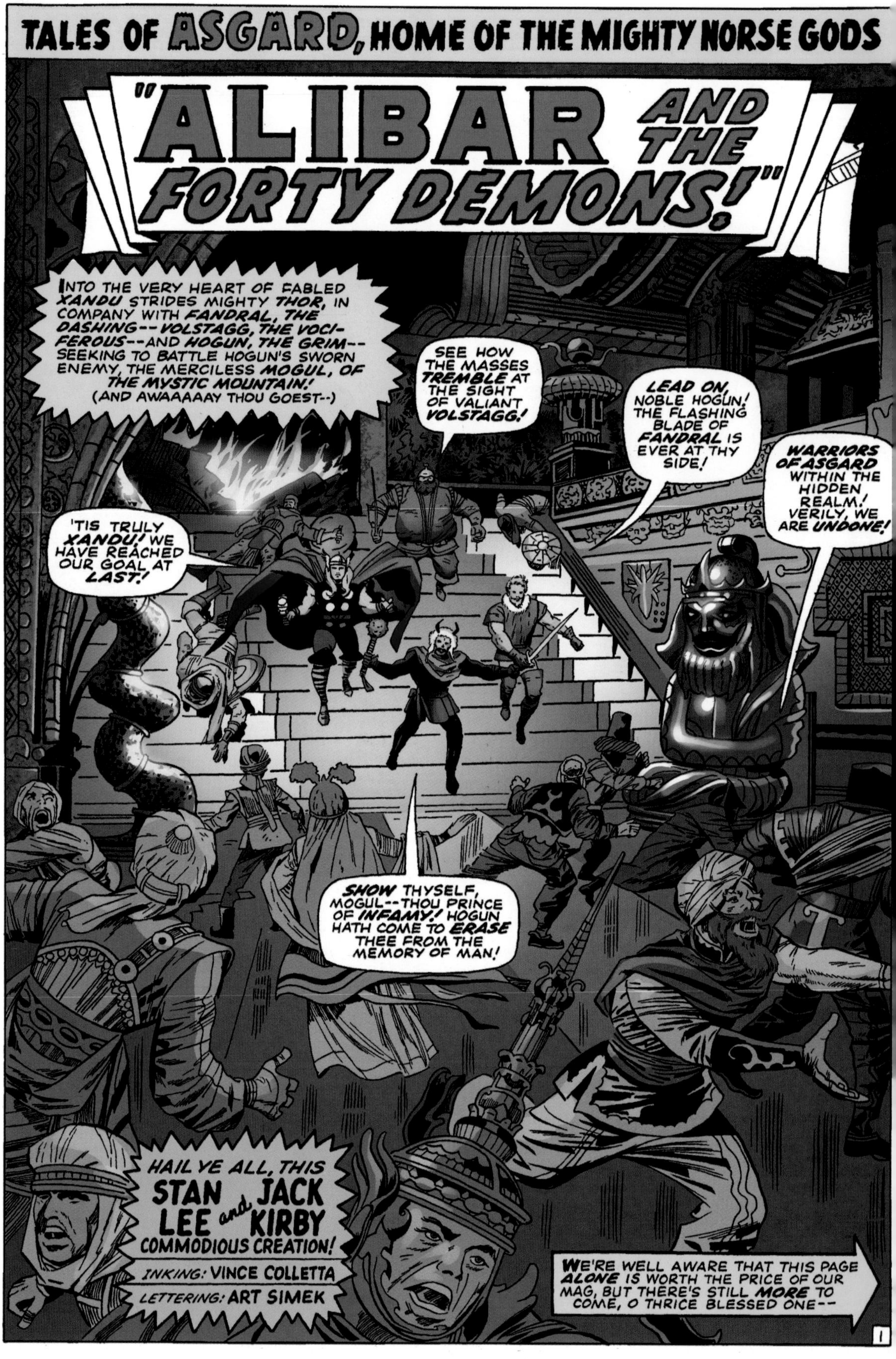
TALES OF ASGARD, HOME OF THE MIGHTY NORSE GODS
"ALIBAR AND THE FORTY DEMONS!"
INTO THE VERY HEART OF FABLED XANDU STRIDES MIGHTY THOR, IN COMPANY WITH FANDRAL, THE DASHING--VOLSTAGG, THE VOCIFEROUS--AND HOGUN, THE GRIM--SEEKING TO BATTLE HOGUN'S SWORN ENEMY, THE MERCILESS MOGUL, OF THE MYSTIC MOUNTAIN! (AND AWAAAAAAY THOU GOEST--)
SEE HOW THE MASSES TREMBLE AT THE SIGHT OF VALIANT VOLSTAGG!
LEAD ON, NOBLE HOGUN! THE FLASHING BLADE OF FANDRAL IS EVER AT THY SIDE!
WARRIORS OF ASGARD WITHIN THE HIDDEN REALM! VERILY, WE ARE UNDONE!
'TIS TRULY XANDU! WE HAVE REACHED OUR GOAL AT LAST!
SHOW THYSELF, MOGUL--THOU PRINCE OF INFAMY! HOGUN HATH COME TO ERASE THEE FROM THE MEMORY OF MAN!
HAIL YE ALL, THIS STAN LEE and JACK KIRBY COMMODIOUS CREATION!
INKING: VINCE COLLETTA
LETTERING: ART SIMEK
WE'RE WELL AWARE THAT THIS PAGE ALONE IS WORTH THE PRICE OF OUR MAG, BUT THERE'S STILL MORE TO COME, O THRICE BLESSED ONE--
1

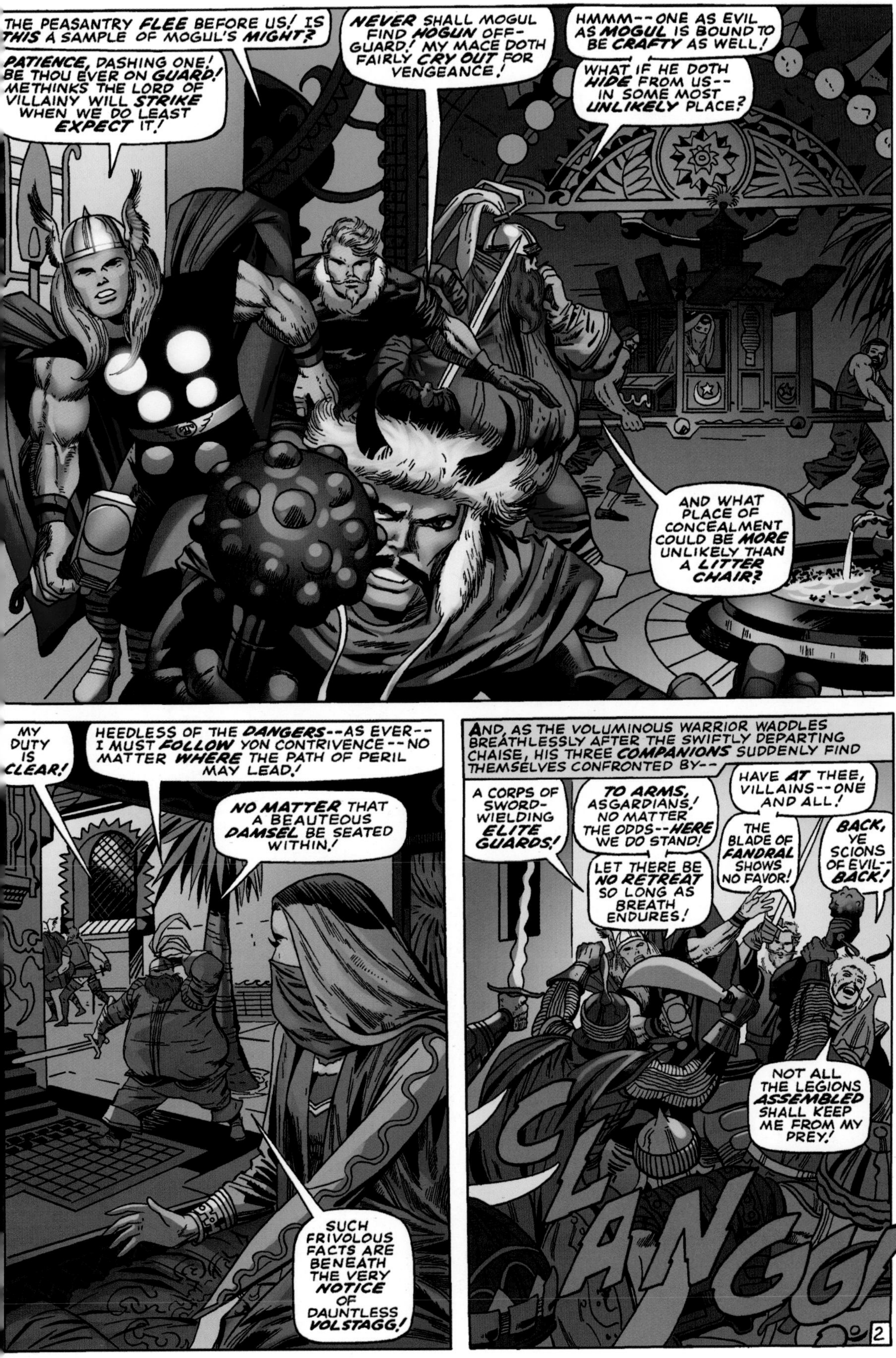
THE PEASANTRY FLEE BEFORE US! IS THIS A SAMPLE OF MOGUL'S MIGHT?
PATIENCE, DASHING ONE! BE THOU EVER ON GUARD! METHINKS THE LORD OF VILLAINY WILL STRIKE WHEN WE DO LEAST EXPECT IT!
NEVER SHALL MOGUL FIND HOGUN OFF-GUARD! MY MACE DOTH FAIRLY CRY OUT FOR VENGEANCE!
HMMM--ONE AS EVIL AS MOGUL IS BOUND TO BE CRAFTY AS WELL!
WHAT IF HE DOTH HIDE FROM US--IN SOME MOST UNLIKELY PLACE?
AND WHAT PLACE OF CONCEALMENT COULD BE MORE UNLIKELY THAN A LITTER CHAIR?
MY DUTY IS CLEAR!
HEEDLESS OF THE DANGERS--AS EVER--I MUST FOLLOW YON CONTRIVENCE--NO MATTER WHERE THE PATH OF PERIL MAY LEAD!
NO MATTER THAT A BEAUTEOUS DAMSEL BE SEATED WITHIN!
SUCH FRIVOLOUS FACTS ARE BENEATH THE VERY NOTICE OF DAUNTLESS VOLSTAGG!
AND, AS THE VOLUMINOUS WARRIOR WADDLES BREATHLESSLY AFTER THE SWIFTLY DEPARTING CHAISE, HIS THREE COMPANIONS SUDDENLY FIND THEMSELVES CONFRONTED BY--
A CORPS OF SWORD-WIELDING ELITE GUARDS!
TO ARMS, ASGARDIANS! NO MATTER THE ODDS--HERE WE DO STAND!
LET THERE BE NO RETREAT SO LONG AS BREATH ENDURES!
HAVE AT THEE, VILLAINS--ONE AND ALL!
THE BLADE OF FANDRAL SHOWS NO FAVOR!
BACK, YE SCIONS OF EVIL--BACK!
NOT ALL THE LEGIONS ASSEMBLED SHALL KEEP ME FROM MY PREY!
CLANGG!
2

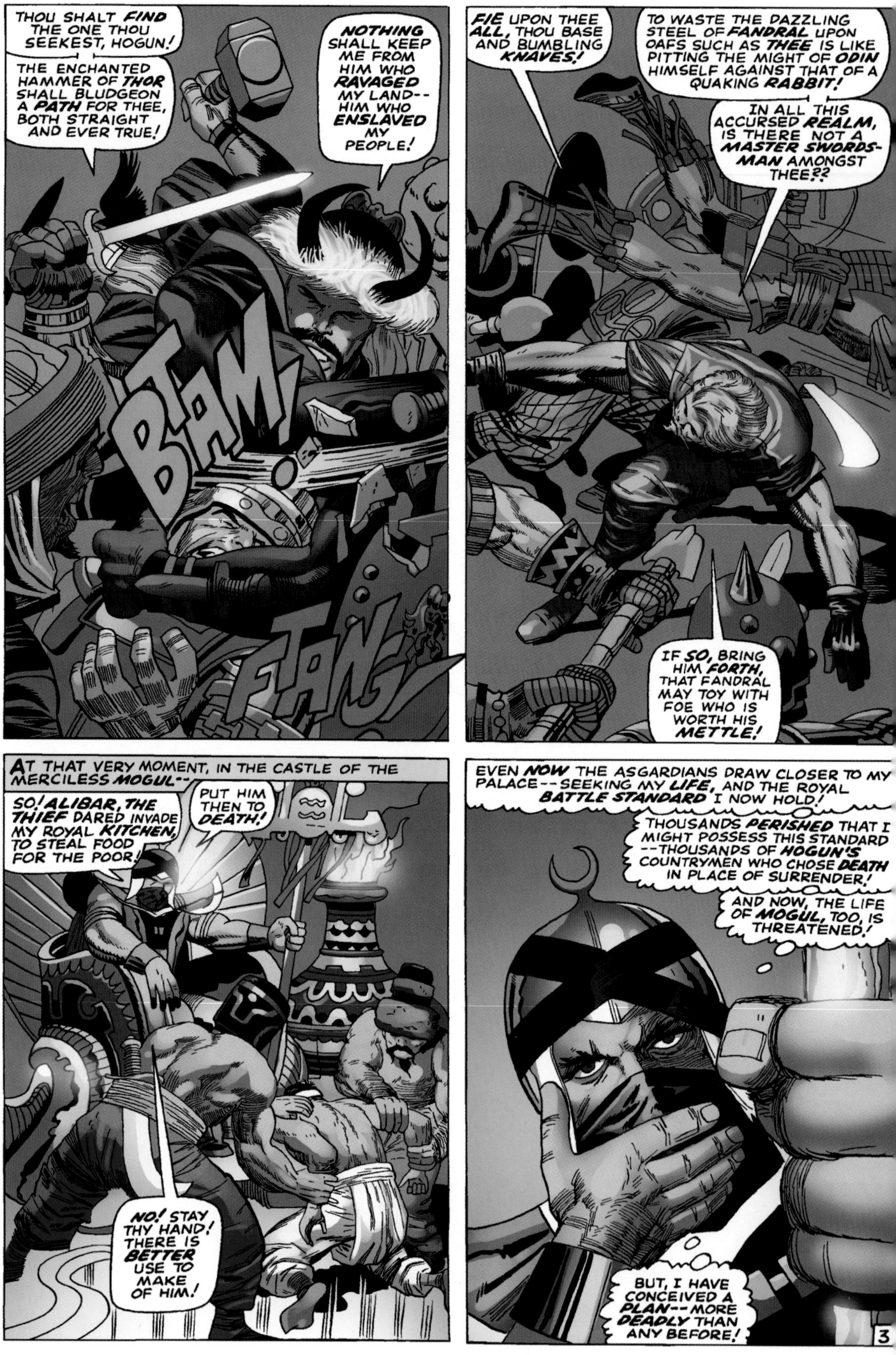

THOU SHALT FIND THE ONE THOU SEEKEST, HOGUN!
THE ENCHANTED HAMMER OF THOR SHALL BLUDGEON A PATH FOR THEE, BOTH STRAIGHT AND EVER TRUE!
NOTHING SHALL KEEP ME FROM HIM WHO RAVAGED MY LAND-- HIM WHO ENSLAVED MY PEOPLE!
BAM!
FTANG
FIE UPON THEE ALL, THOU BASE AND BUMBLING KNAVES!
TO WASTE THE DAZZLING STEEL OF FANDRAL UPON OAFS SUCH AS THEE IS LIKE PITTING THE MIGHT OF ODIN HIMSELF AGAINST THAT OF A QUAKING RABBIT!
IN ALL THIS ACCURSED REALM, IS THERE NOT A MASTER SWORDS-MAN AMONGST THEE??
IF SO, BRING HIM FORTH, THAT FANDRAL MAY TOY WITH FOE WHO IS WORTH HIS METTLE!
AT THAT VERY MOMENT, IN THE CASTLE OF THE MERCILESS MOGUL--
SO! ALIBAR, THE THIEF DARED INVADE MY ROYAL KITCHEN, TO STEAL FOOD FOR THE POOR!
PUT HIM THEN TO DEATH!
NO! STAY THY HAND! THERE IS BETTER USE TO MAKE OF HIM!
EVEN NOW THE ASGARDIANS DRAW CLOSER TO MY PALACE--SEEKING MY LIFE, AND THE ROYAL BATTLE STANDARD I NOW HOLD!
THOUSANDS PERISHED THAT I MIGHT POSSESS THIS STANDARD --THOUSANDS OF HOGUN'S COUNTRYMEN WHO CHOSE DEATH IN PLACE OF SURRENDER!
AND NOW, THE LIFE OF MOGUL, TOO, IS THREATENED!
BUT, I HAVE CONCEIVED A PLAN--MORE DEADLY THAN ANY BEFORE!
3

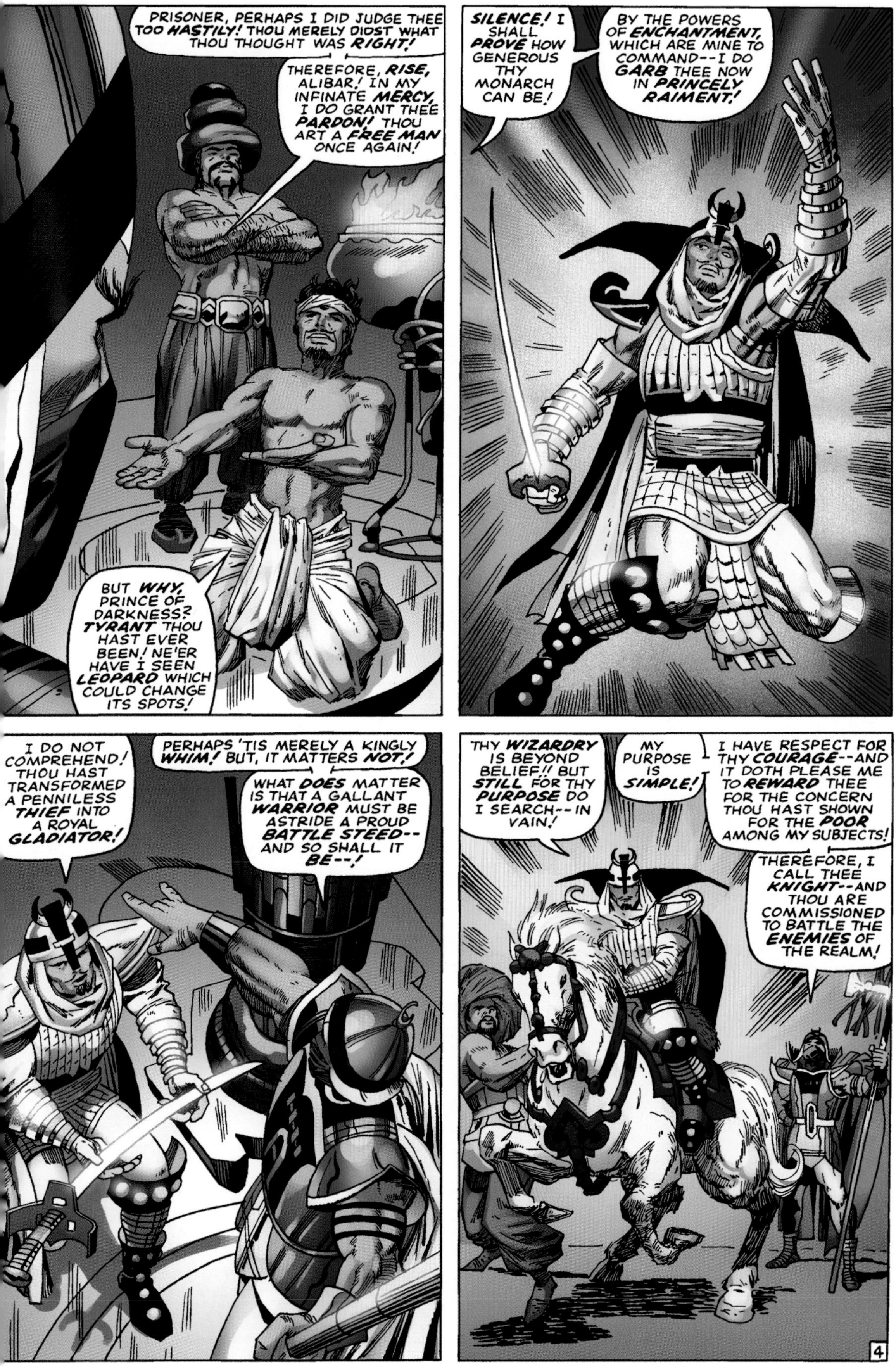
PRISONER, PERHAPS I DID JUDGE THEE TOO HASTILY! THOU MERELY DIDST WHAT THOU THOUGHT WAS RIGHT!
THEREFORE, RISE, ALIBAR! IN MY INFINATE MERCY, I DO GRANT THEE PARDON! THOU ART A FREE MAN ONCE AGAIN!
BUT WHY, PRINCE OF DARKNESS? TYRANT THOU HAST EVER BEEN! NE'ER HAVE I SEEN LEOPARD WHICH COULD CHANGE ITS SPOTS!
SILENCE! I SHALL PROVE HOW GENEROUS THY MONARCH CAN BE!
BY THE POWERS OF ENCHANTMENT, WHICH ARE MINE TO COMMAND--I DO GARB THEE NOW IN PRINCELY RAIMENT!
I DO NOT COMPREHEND! THOU HAST TRANSFORMED A PENNILESS THIEF INTO A ROYAL GLADIATOR!
PERHAPS 'TIS MERELY A KINGLY WHIM! BUT, IT MATTERS NOT!
WHAT DOES MATTER IS THAT A GALLANT WARRIOR MUST BE ASTRIDE A PROUD BATTLE STEED--AND SO SHALL IT BE--!
THY WIZARDRY IS BEYOND BELIEF!! BUT STILL FOR THY PURPOSE DO I SEARCH--IN VAIN!
MY PURPOSE IS SIMPLE!
I HAVE RESPECT FOR THY COURAGE--AND IT DOTH PLEASE ME TO REWARD THEE FOR THE CONCERN THOU HAST SHOWN FOR THE POOR AMONG MY SUBJECTS!
THEREFORE, I CALL THEE KNIGHT--AND THOU ARE COMMISSIONED TO BATTLE THE ENEMIES OF THE REALM!
4

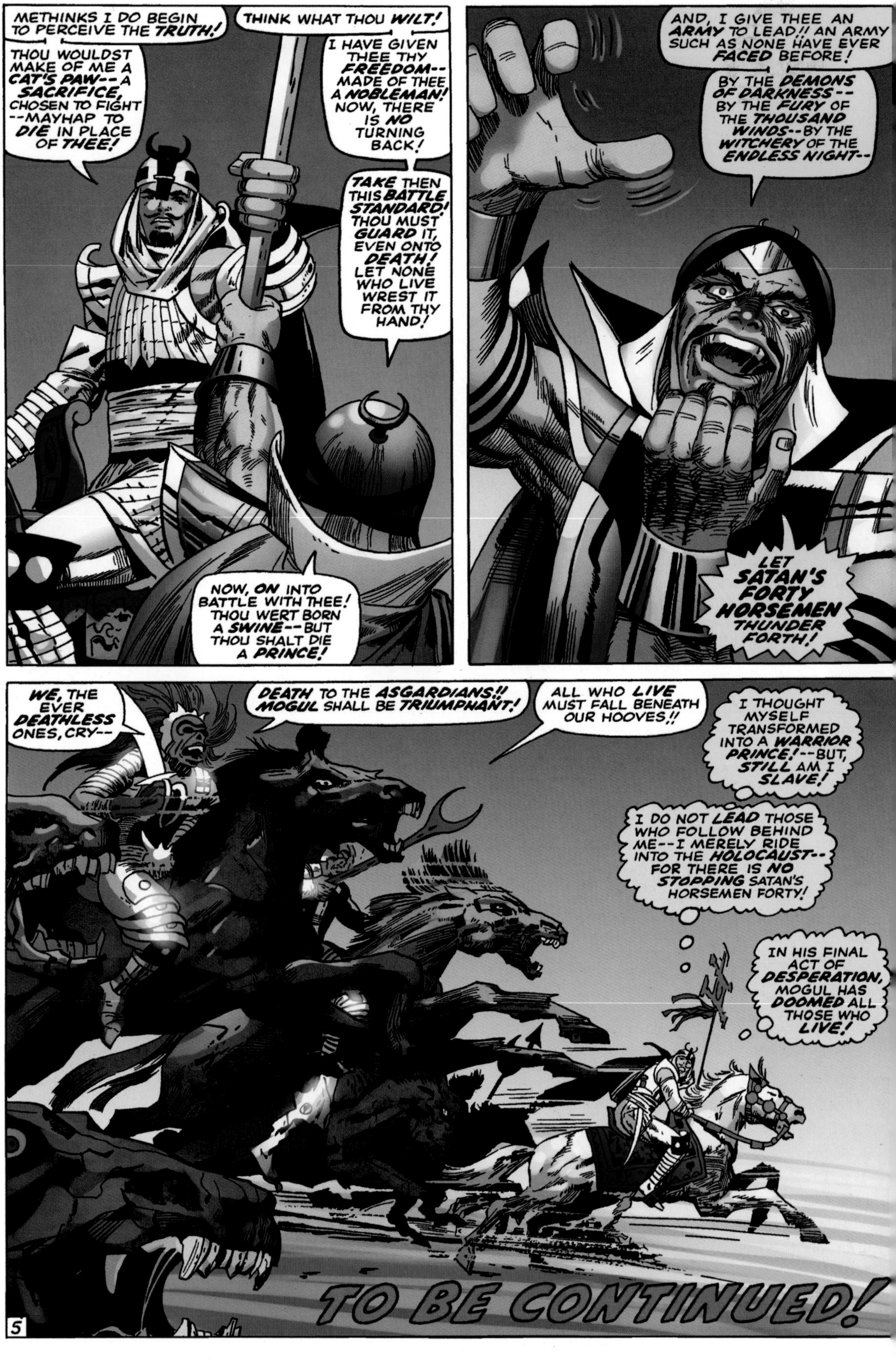
METHINKS I DO BEGIN TO PERCEIVE THE TRUTH!
THINK WHAT THOU WILT!
THOU WOULDST MAKE OF ME A CAT'S PAW--A SACRIFICE, CHOSEN TO FIGHT --MAYHAP TO DIE IN PLACE OF THEE!
I HAVE GIVEN THEE THY FREEDOM-- MADE OF THEE A NOBLEMAN! NOW, THERE IS NO TURNING BACK!
TAKE THEN THIS BATTLE STANDARD! THOU MUST GUARD IT, EVEN ONTO DEATH! LET NONE WHO LIVE WREST IT FROM THY HAND!
NOW, ON INTO BATTLE WITH THEE! THOU WERT BORN A SWINE--BUT THOU SHALT DIE A PRINCE!
AND, I GIVE THEE AN ARMY TO LEAD!! AN ARMY SUCH AS NONE HAVE EVER FACED BEFORE!
BY THE DEMONS OF DARKNESS--BY THE FURY OF THE THOUSAND WINDS--BY THE WITCHERY OF THE ENDLESS NIGHT--
LET SATAN'S FORTY HORSEMEN THUNDER FORTH!
WE, THE EVER DEATHLESS ONES, CRY--
DEATH TO THE ASGARDIANS!! MOGUL SHALL BE TRIUMPHANT!
ALL WHO LIVE MUST FALL BENEATH OUR HOOVES!!
I THOUGHT MYSELF TRANSFORMED INTO A WARRIOR PRINCE!--BUT, STILL AM I SLAVE!
I DO NOT LEAD THOSE WHO FOLLOW BEHIND ME--I MERELY RIDE INTO THE HOLOCAUST--FOR THERE IS NO STOPPING SATAN'S HORSEMEN FORTY!
IN HIS FINAL ACT OF DESPERATION, MOGUL HAS DOOMED ALL THOSE WHO LIVE!
TO BE CONTINUED!
5

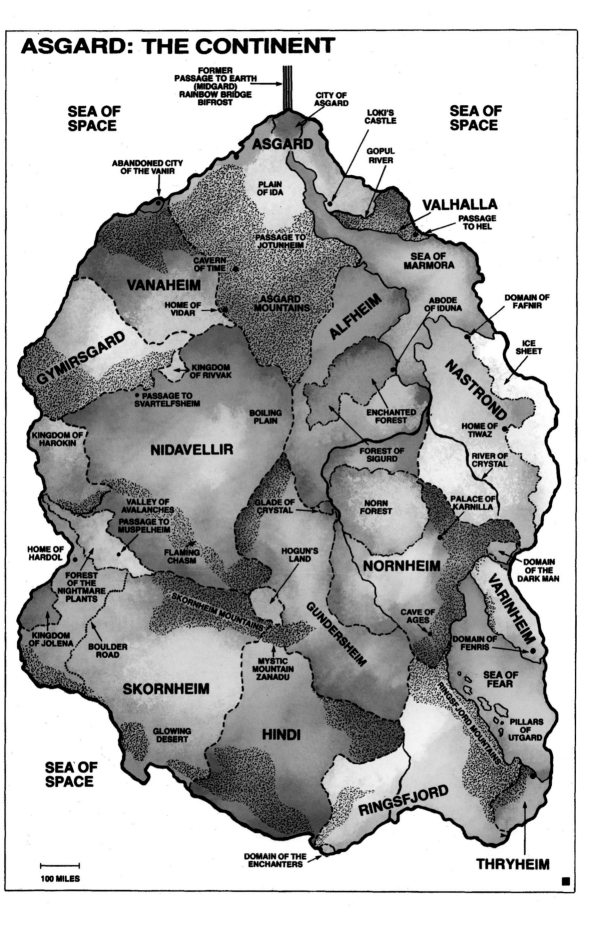

ASGARD: THE CONTINENT

FORMER PASSAGE TO EARTH (MIDGARD) RAINBOW BRIDGE BIFROST

CITY OF ASGARD

LOKI'S CASTLE

GOPUL RIVER

SEA OF SPACE

SEA OF SPACE

ASGARD

VALHALLA

PASSAGE TO HEL

ABANDONED CITY OF THE VANIR

PLAIN OF IDA

PASSAGE TO JOTUNHEIM

CAVERN OF TIME

SEA OF MARMORA

ABODE OF IDUNA

DOMAIN OF FAFNIR

VANAHEIM

ALFHEIM

HOME OF VIDAR

ASGARD MOUNTAINS

ICE SHEET

GYMIRSGARD

NASTROND

KINGDOM OF RIVVAK

PASSAGE TO SVARTELFSHEIM

BOILING PLAIN

ENCHANTED FOREST

HOME OF TIWAZ

KINGDOM OF HAROKIN

FOREST OF SIGURD

RIVER OF CRYSTAL

NIDAVELLIR

GLADE OF CRYSTAL

NORN FOREST

PALACE OF KARNILLA

VALLEY OF AVALANCHES

PASSAGE TO MUSPELHEIM

HOGUN'S LAND

HOME OF HARDOL

FLAMING CHASM

NORNHEIM

DOMAIN OF THE DARK MAN

FOREST OF THE NIGHTMARE PLANTS

SKORNHEIM MOUNTAINS

GUNDERSHEIM

VARINHEIM

CAVE OF AGES

DOMAIN OF FENRIS

KINGDOM OF JOLENA

BOULDER ROAD

MYSTIC MOUNTAIN ZANADU

SEA OF FEAR

SKORNHEIM

HINDI

RINGSFJORD MOUNTAINS

PILLARS OF UTGARD

SEA OF SPACE

GLOWING DESERT

RINGSFJORD

100 MILES

DOMAIN OF THE ENCHANTERS

THRYHEIM

ASGARD: THE NINE WORLDS

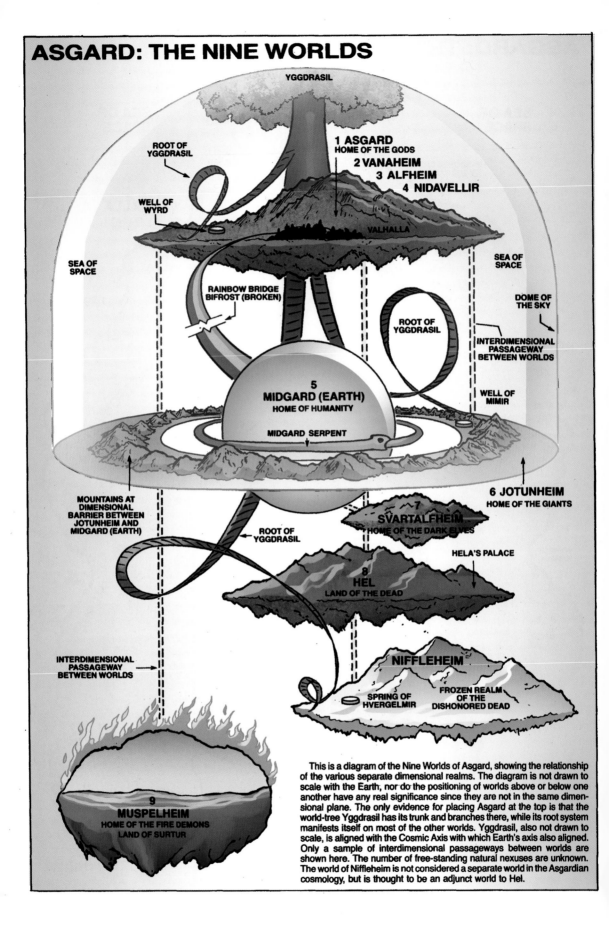

YGGDRASIL

ROOT OF YGGDRASIL

1 ASGARD
HOME OF THE GODS
2 VANAHEIM
3 ALFHEIM
4 NIDAVELLIR

WELL OF WYRD

VALHALLA

SEA OF SPACE

SEA OF SPACE

RAINBOW BRIDGE BIFROST (BROKEN)

ROOT OF YGGDRASIL

DOME OF THE SKY

INTERDIMENSIONAL PASSAGEWAY BETWEEN WORLDS

WELL OF MIMIR

5 MIDGARD (EARTH)
HOME OF HUMANITY

MIDGARD SERPENT

MOUNTAINS AT DIMENSIONAL BARRIER BETWEEN JOTUNHEIM AND MIDGARD (EARTH)

6 JOTUNHEIM
HOME OF THE GIANTS

ROOT OF YGGDRASIL

7 SVARTALFHEIM
HOME OF THE DARK ELVES

HELA'S PALACE

8 HEL
LAND OF THE DEAD

INTERDIMENSIONAL PASSAGEWAY BETWEEN WORLDS

NIFFLEHEIM

SPRING OF HVERGELMIR

FROZEN REALM OF THE DISHONORED DEAD

9 MUSPELHEIM
HOME OF THE FIRE DEMONS
LAND OF SURTUR

This is a diagram of the Nine Worlds of Asgard, showing the relationship of the various separate dimensional realms. The diagram is not drawn to scale with the Earth, nor do the positioning of worlds above or below one another have any real significance since they are not in the same dimensional plane. The only evidence for placing Asgard at the top is that the world-tree Yggdrasil has its trunk and branches there, while its root system manifests itself on most of the other worlds. Yggdrasil, also not drawn to scale, is aligned with the Cosmic Axis with which Earth's axis also aligned. Only a sample of interdimensional passageways between worlds are shown here. The number of free-standing natural nexuses are unknown. The world of Niffleheim is not considered a separate world in the Asgardian cosmology, but is thought to be an adjunct world to Hel.